Sexton Blake's Blunder

by G. H. Teed

First published in the Union Jack Library magazine,
Series 2, No. 981, 29 July, 1922.

Illustrated by H. M. Lewis

Stillwoods Edition

Stillwoods.Blogspot.Ca

Catalogue Information:
Title: Sexton Blake's Blunder
Author: G. H. Teed (1881-1938)
First published anonymously in the Union Jack Library magazine, Series 2, No. 981, 29 July, 1922.
Illustrated by H. M. Lewis
This Edition by: Stillwoods, 2021, (Doug Frizzle)
ISBN Canada: 978-1-989788-53-0
Blog: Stillwoods.Blogspot.Ca
Author Blog: http://ghteed.blogspot.com/
Storefront: http://www.lulu.com/spotlight/lulubook22

Keywords: Sexton Blake, British fictional detective, Tinker, Dr. Huxton Rymer, Yvonne Cartier

The library of Teed's stories increases almost daily. Check at the bookstore link above for the latest arrivals. /drf

Cautionary Note: This series of books by Stillwoods are intended to make the stories of G. H. Teed, born in New Brunswick, Canada, available to collectors and researchers. The editor, or rather digitizer has not altered the original publication.

This story may contain language and racial terms that are not appropriate to today. I apologize for them; I know that the author was using his voice to excite and entertain an adventurous English audience. These works were published from 82 to 110 years ago. Most every work has characters of redeeming ethnicity within.

I hope you enjoy and share these stories; I have.
Doug Frizzle

**Introducing Sexton Blake, Tinker, Mademoiselle Yvonne —
and Dr. Huxton Rymer.** Complete in this number, and specially
written to appeal to readers of all ages.

This is the second of the brilliant author's Dr. Huxton Rymer
stories. The first appeared last week, and the third will follow this.
Though each is complete in itself, you are recommended to obtain
and read the lot, for the three form as fine a trilogy as the U. J. has
had for a very long time—and that is saying something, for the U. J.
leads in the realm of detective fiction, of course.

The series includes:
The Case of the Winfield Handicap
Sexton Blake's Blunder
The Affair of the Rickshaw Coolie
All have been digitized and are available! /drf

1922 Packard /drf

SEXTON BLAKE'S BLUNDER.

Introducing **SEXTON BLAKE, TINKER, Mademoiselle YVONNE**—and Dr. **HUXTON RYMER.** Complete in this number, and specially written to appeal to readers of all ages.

This is the second of the brilliant author's Dr. HUXTON RYMER stories. The first appeared last week, and the third will follow this. Though each is complete in itself, you are recommended to obtain and read the lot, for the three form as fine a trilogy as the U. J. has had for a very long time—and that is saying something, for the U. J. leads in the realm of ∴ detective fiction, of course. ∴

Prologue. A Painful Duty—Where is Whidden Crane?—Sexton Blake an Interested Party—He Makes an Offer —Which is Accepted with Acclamation.

"AND now, ladies and gentlemen, I regret that is about all I can tell you to-day of this regrettable occurrence. The accountants are dealing with the books as rapidly as possible and expect to be able to issue a more detailed statement in a few days. But I am afraid I can offer little hope in that.

"As far as we can see at present, we have been very seriously duped by our missing general manager, and, as I stated before, the amount with which he has absconded would seem to be in the neighbourhood of £150,000 —all in cash or negotiable Government bonds.

"My fellow directors all agreed that it was wiser to call this extraordinary general meeting to see if some scheme of reconstruction could be agreed upon. Failing that, it only remains for us to apply to the official receiver for a winding-up order.

"I hope, therefore, that you will give the matter your very serious attention. Until the heavy defalcations of him whom we trusted so implicitly, the condition of the company was sound, and it is my opinion that a way might be found out by which we could put it back into the same healthy state after a few years. But, as I have already said, it is for your decision, as any such scheme would necessarily entail further cash sacrifices on your part.

"Before we take a vote I shall be pleased to answer, as far as possible, any questions any of you may wish to put to me."

Sir Frederick Cameron, the speaker, paused and glanced at the men and women grouped round the long table at the head of which he stood. He had just completed a speech, in which it had been his duty to make a very painful speech. He had had to inform his fellow shareholders that, owing to the heavy defalcations of the managing director and his subsequent disappearance, the affairs of the Universal Machine Company were in a very critical state.

In fact, so badly crippled were the finances that, unless a scheme of reconstruction could be arranged, it mean bankruptcy and, for many of the shareholders, ruin.

That was the fact which those men and women had to face, and while each and everyone must have felt an intense anger against the absconder, it was remarkable that they showed such restraint.

In response to the chairman's offer, a gentleman who was seated near the door rose.

"Before we go to a vote, Mr. Chairman, I should like to ask what is the present position of the company regarding future business?" he said. "It would seem that this is an important factor in considering any scheme of reconstruction."

"That is so," answered the chairman. "I am glad you have asked the question. The position of the company in that respect is excellent. Our London factory is working at full pressure as well as our branch factory at Manchester.

"I am informed by the sales manager that the company has in hand orders for sufficient machines to keep both factories running at full pressure for the next seven months.

"Further, the prospects of new orders are excellent, and are being received by every mail from all over the world. We are making one of the best oil engines in the world, and it would be a pity if the company were to go into liquidation just when business is beginning to pick up."

The inquirer thanked the chairman and sat down. Then, after a short pause, another gentleman rose.

"I wish to ask a question, Mr. Chairman," he said, "and it has not a very direct bearing on your remarks. At the same time, I am sure, there are many of my fellow shareholders who will agree with me."

"I shall do my best to reply, sir."

"Thank you. As I understand things from the very frank statement you have made, and for which I am sure we are all indebted to you, it appears that our late general manager, Whidden Crane, has embezzled funds of the company amounting to approximately £150,000?"

"That is so, sir."

"I gather, further, that he disappeared some six days ago, and that nothing has been heard of him since."

"Quite right."

"Has the matter been put in the hands of the police?"

"Yes, sir. The police were communicated with to-day and, I understand, have issued a warrant. This would have been done before, but it was not until yesterday that the accountants knew definitely that the defalcations were the work of Crane, although they held strong suspicions!"

"Thank you, Mr. Chairman. And now, while I am sure the police will use every effort to discover the whereabouts of the absconder, it has occurred to me that we might take further steps. I notice among us to-day a gentleman who, we all know, is very eminent in his profession, and who, it appears, is also a fellow-sufferer with us.

"I refer, sir, to Mr. Sexton Blake, who is seated near you. If Mr. Blake's engagements will permit, would it not be advisable to retain his services? I feel sure that if anyone can run this scoundrel to earth Mr. Blake is the one to do it. And he may succeed in recovering some of the stolen funds."

As the speaker bowed and sat down, there was an ever-growing murmur of approval round the table, and soon several persons were calling the name of Blake. The chairman held up his hand.

"I am in entire agreement with the suggestion of the gentleman who has just spoken," he said. "It seems to me that it would be a most excellent thing if Mr. Blake could be persuaded to take up this inquiry for us."

Then he turned to Blake. "What do you say, Mr. Blake?"

Sexton Blake, who had been a silent spectator of the proceedings, rose and smiled at the gentleman who had made the suggestion.

"For myself, I am in entire agreement with the suggestion that the man whom we all trusted should be run down as quickly as possible. It will be no easy matter, for he is well provided with funds, and has already had time to put a good many miles between himself and London, if he has been able to overcome passport difficulties.

"That we can only know after making inquiries. But, if it is the wish of the shareholders that I should take up the case. I shall be happy to do so, on the distinct understanding that I receive no fee!

"I am personally interested in the affair, and I do not think it would be fair in the present straitened circumstances of the company, for the finances to be put to any greater strain than is absolutely necessary. Business on which I am at present engaged may take me across to the Continent for a day or two; but, before I go, I shall start my inquiries, that is, if you wish me to do so."

As the famous criminologist sat down half a dozen persons rose to speak. Sir Frederick Cameron smiled and held up his hand.

"I think I may speak for us all," he said. "I am sure we are very grateful to Mr. Blake for what we all must feel is a most magnanimous offer, and, I believe, I speak for each one when I say that we accept, gratefully!"

The chorus of "hear, hears" more than confirmed his words, and, rising, Blake thanked them, adding that he would use his very best efforts on their behalf. Following that, the question of reconstruction was put to the vote, and when the tally was taken, it was found that an overwhelming majority had voted in favour of contributing to some such scheme, so that the company might be saved.

As the meeting broke up, the assembled shareholders crowded round Blake to shake his hand and thank him personally for his generous offer. Practically everyone present availed himself of the opportunity; but a close observer might have noticed that one man who had been present at the meeting did not do so! Instead, he took the opportunity to slip quietly from the room, and five minutes later he was boarding a bus bound for the East End of London.

(End of Prologue.)

" If it is the wish of the shareholders that I should take up the case," said Sexton Blake, " I shall be happy to do so on the distinct understanding that I receive no fee, in view of the fact that I am a shareholder myself." (*Prologue.*)

The door-handle turned noiselessly, and a charming apparition stole into Sexton Blake's consulting-room. Tinker jumped with surprise as her hand was laid gently on his shoulder. (*Chapter 1.*)

The First Chapter.   Tinker Receives a Blow —A Fair Sympathiser —The Explanation of Blake's Curious Conduct —An Invitation — And Its Acceptance.

"I QUITE understand, mademoiselle. Pray do not apologise." Sexton Blake, eminent criminologist and prober of a thousand secrets, snapped the receiver on its hook and turned sharply away from the telephone, a certain look of icy displeasure on his stern features.

"As we are going round by Queen Anne's Gate, we had better hurry, guv'nor," cheerfully called Tinker from the door where he stood struggling into his motor-coat.

"We are not going round by Queen Anne's Gate."

"W-what?" Tinker paused for a moment in sheer surprise at something he had seldom before heard in his chief's voice. "I —I thought —"

"If you would think less and act more it would be better for both of us, my lad," said Blake coldly, as, with a savage gleam in his eye, he swung out of the consulting-room at Baker Street.

Tinker flinched as though he had been struck.

"Well, are you coming?" called Blake gruffly over his shoulder.

"I —I don't think so, guv'nor. I —I'd rather not, if you will excuse me," answered his young assistant in an expressionless tone, letting his coat slip from him as he spoke.

A door banged sharply, and presently he heard the throbbing of the Grey Panther's powerful engine till the sound merged in the roar of London's ceaseless traffic.

"If you'd think less and act more!" repeated Tinker aloud, entering the consulting-room and leaning heavily on the big desk, an expression of blank dismay and hurt wonder on his honest young face.

Blake's sharp words had hit him hard, more especially as —rack his mind as he would —he could remember no act of his that seemed to justify the cutting reproof.

"Why? Why? —Why?" murmured Tinker. "What have I done? Oh, hang it all! What's the good of anything? The guv'nor —the guv'nor, of all men —to hand me such a rotten one! Oh!" And Tinker sank into Blake's empty seat, his head going down on his arms spread out before him.

His world was toppling round him —or seemed to be.

The shrill ring of the telephone-bell brought him listlessly to his feet. He walked over to the instrument and took down the receiver.

"Hallo! Yes. Oh, it's you, mademoiselle. Er —no, I'm not going to the countess' fete. Yes, the guv'nor has gone. I know we were coming round to pick you up. I don't know, mademoiselle. No, I'd rather not, thank you. I —I don't feel very fit this afternoon. Oh, nothing at all, I assure you."

After exchanging a few more words, Tinker hung up the receiver and strolled aimlessly about the room, taking refuge eventually in one of the comfortable leather chairs by the hearth. With his elbows on his knees, and his chin on his closed knuckles, he sat gazing into the empty fireplace, the exposed ironwork of which was due to Blake's firmness about Mrs. Bardell's annual desire to replace the cheery fires of the winter months with outbursts of pleated paper at the approach of summer.

Silence reigned in the room, broken only by the solemn regular tick of the clock on the mantel.

Tinker's thoughts were travelling far back down the years, waking from their corners many long-past incidents of peril shared with Blake, calling to mind each treasured proof of his chief's affectionate trust in him. No one knew better than Tinker what he owed to the kindly, generous man who had done so much for him.

So occupied was the boy with his thoughts that he did not hear the door bell ring, or the sound of voices as someone was admitted, and subsequently a soft footfall approaching the consulting-room.

Presently the handle of the door turned noiselessly, and a charming apparition stole gently in.

Mademoiselle Yvonne Cartier stood looking uncertainly at Tinker's unconscious back.

Her blonde beauty, always arresting, seemed to bring a sudden radiance into the brown quietness of Blake's consulting-room. The soft grey motor-coat she wore was thrown back, revealing a dainty toilette in that pleasing shade beloved by and named after the great painter, Nattier. A small but fascinating hat of the "poke bonnet" variety, in colour matching the eyes and frock below, completed the charming ensemble Yvonne had hoped would evoke the accustomed gleam of approval in a pair of eyes whose approval were more to her than that of any others.

The despondency of Tinker's attitude moved her to step swiftly across the room and lay one shapely arm about his bowed shoulders.

Tinker jumped with surprise. "Mademoiselle!" he gasped. "I never heard you come in! How jolly seeing you!"

"Now, tell me!" said Yvonne, when she had settled herself in the easy-chair on the other side of the fireplace. "Is —is anything wrong, Tinker? Is Mr. Blake upset about anything?" And as she asked this question Yvonne blushed slightly and looked in troubled fashion at the floor.

"Yes —no! I don't know what it can be," confided Tinker, his brow wrinkling thoughtfully.

"But something is the matter?" persisted Yvonne softly.

"I've been sitting here for at least half an hour trying to figure out what it can be," confessed the lad. "But it has me' beat. I—I've never had the guv'nor speak to me as he did this afternoon. Nothing much, but it was the way he said it. As if —as if he really meant it—" And Tinker broke off ruefully.

Yvonne clenched her little gloved hand.

"I —I'm afraid it is my fault, Tinker," she said in a low voice.

"Wha-at? Your fault?" Tinker looked at Yvonne in amazement. "How do you mean, mademoiselle?"

"I'll tell you," said the girl, raising beautiful, troubled eyes to his. "It is about to-night. I was to have dined with you and gone to a theatre and supper afterwards, as you know. I —I rang up Mr. Blake this afternoon to explain why I was obliged to break my appointment—"

"Oh! Aren't you coming, then?" cried Tinker blankly.

"No. You see, Tinker, years ago an old friend of my mother's made me promise to give him the first evening he found himself in London again. Well, he arrived to-day from the East, and held me to my promise. I felt it impossible to make an excuse, and I knew —at least, I thought I knew —that if I explained Mr. Blake would understand—"

"To-night was to be a very special night," interrupted Tinker. "The guv'nor had planned to take you, as a surprise, to hear the great Russian violinist, Premyslav—"

"Premyslav in London!" exclaimed Yvonne.

"Only for two days," Tinker told her. "The guv'nor had cards from him this morning. He has asked a few people to his rooms at the Venetia to-night to hear him play. He has never forgotten what the guv'nor did for him three years ago, you know."

Yvonne looked as she felt —deeply disappointed.

"I should have loved that. I have never heard him. But, still, Tinker, I could not break my promise to my mother's friend, Paul Brabazon."

"Not Brabazon, the writer?" asked Tinker quickly.

Yvonne nodded.

"Yes, do you know him?"

"Only by sight. But —but he is not very old," bluntly observed the lad.

"He is not at all old. Just about— about Mr. Blake's age, I think. But, Tinker, you have not told me why you did not come round to pick me up this afternoon. It was not definitely arranged, but I thought—"

"So did I," said Tinker, stirring uneasily.

Yvonne's eyes looked more troubled than ever,

"Won't you come to the fete with me, Tinker?" she asked softly. "I —I'm all alone."

Tinker stood up and reached for his cap.

"Thank you, mademoiselle, I shall be delighted to!"

SEXTON BLAKE was a man of his word. Otherwise, it can confidently be stated, had he not promised, nothing could have induced him to attend the Countess of Dewsberry's fete in aid of a well-known charity that afternoon.

He was not in the mood to mingle with a laughing, chattering crowd, purchase useless trifles for fabulous sums, or engage in vapid nothings with a host of trivial acquaintances. His keen mind, occupied with the solving of a certain mystery that seemed to elude him time and again, was ill-attuned to the atmosphere of such a time-wasting triviality.

On top of his professional anxieties had come the sudden disappointment in Yvonne's unexpected withdrawal of her promise to dine with him that night.

Jarred and irritated, it is to be feared Blake read into her alteration of their plans a waning of that subtly sweet friendship he had come to prize more highly than he himself realised.

Therefore, when he caught sight of Yvonne and Tinker making the round of the stalls about three-quarters of an hour, after his own arrival, Blake refrained from joining them, as he most certainly would have done twenty-four hours earlier, and kept in the small crowd that formed his pretty hostess' train.

The young Countess of Dewsberry was greatly flattered by the interest the famous man seemed to be taking in her pet charity. She was also not averse to practising a few of her pretty arts on him, though well aware that Sexton Blake had never been known to show a preference for any woman's society —save one, perhaps.

It was whispered that the beautiful Mademoiselle Cartier had as much of the great detective's admiration and friendship as he was capable of giving any woman, for the sex, it was known, played little part in his life.

It did not escape Yvonne's notice that the countess was singling Blake out for a good deal of arch attention, nor did she fail to realise that Blake was deliberately avoiding Tinker and herself.

Her proud little chin took a decidedly upward tilt, and very soon she permitted a small court to gather round her. No one seeing the beautiful girl, or hearing her rippling laughter, could have guessed for a fleeting moment the pain that was gripping at her brave and tender heart.

Yvonne played her part gallantly. Never had she seemed more dazzling or bewitching than now. Nor did she dream how the sight of her, apparently enjoying the homage of the little crowd that had gathered round her, put the last touch to Blake's concealed ill-humour with the world.

As the countess' party showed a tendency to join Yvonne's cavalcade, Blake realised that what he had been endeavouring to avoid—namely, a meeting with Yvonne—would inevitably come about. His hurt pride shrank from further proof of her indifference to the claims of their long friendship. A fresh recruit to her troop of admirers in the well-set-up person of Paul Brabazon—the man with whom she was dining that night, instead of with himself, as arranged—sent a curious wave of unreasoning resentment over him.

He turned aside sharply, making for the nearest retreat in sight, which happened to be a little tent hung with dark Eastern shawls. A small sign dangled before the entrance: "Isolte, Psychist."

Blake thrust aside the draperies that veiled the doorway, and, entering, found himself in complete darkness.

The scent of sandalwood was wafted to his nostrils, transporting his thoughts to the insidious mystery of far-off Eastern bazaars. He advanced slowly towards a tiny flame which suddenly appeared at one end of the tent. It grew steadily brighter, until he saw that it came from a copper brazier which hung above a small platform that was covered with heavy black velvet. He stepped upon the dais and found before him a table, also covered with black velvet, and in the centre of which was a large sphere of flawless crystal.

Then his eyes lifted, and on the other side of the table he saw a countenance looming pallidly over a shadowy, bulky form, the swell of the cheekbones lighted up into flickering half-tones by the wavering flame of the brazier.

A thin voice bade him welcome.

Blake bowed, smiling grimly to himself as he did so.

"You have come from afar." chanted the voice, "from going up and down the earth. A great name is yours —one to conjure with."

Blake bowed again sardonically. It was true that he had but recently returned from one of his frequent trips abroad.

"What does one do next, madam?" he asked resignedly. "I should be happier sitting, if I may. This tent is rather low."

"Be seated, Signor Blake," said the voice, with dignity.

Sexton Blake sent a keen glance into the shadows that enveloped Isolte.

He had met with so many instances of a seemingly inexplicable nature, the solutions of which had proved on investigation to be exceedingly simple, that his curiosity to know how the so-called "psychist" was aware of his identity was faded almost as soon as it was roused. Beside which, Blake, modest man as he was, could hardly ignore the fact that he was bound to be well known to a vast circle of persons whose very existence he was unaware of.

He took the somewhat high chair indicated by Isolte, and waited.

"Let the signor place his hand in mine," said the psychist. "I will then lift the curtain that obscures the way before him."

Blake obediently extended his arm across the table, and felt his hand taken into a firm clasp. Not many moments elapsed before Isolte began to speak.

"The signor is a man of many friends and some enemies. There are those who plan and plot to do you ill, there are others to stand by you loyally. Cunning and greed I see working in the darkness. I see evil working against you, a pitfall laid for your feet. Danger—danger lurks before you. Signor, beware! The red mist of anger against a beloved one blinds your eyes."

Blake laughed.

"Pardon me, madame, please continue; I promise not to offend again."

Isolte released his hand.

"It is impossible, signor. Come, try the crystal."

The detective drew the great transparent globe towards him, and bent over it with amused interest.

The moments went by in silence. Blake and the psychist sat facing each other, with the crystal between on the black surface of the draped table.

Presently Blake was mildly interested to observe a cloudiness sweep into the clear depths of the crystal. Dim shadows appeared to be grouping in indistinct fashion beneath his steady concentrated gaze.

With a faint stirring of curiosity he saw the vision resolve itself into what appeared to be a group of men and women seated round a very large table. He bent lower to try and distinguish the features of some of those there, but before he could do so the vision had melted into a swirl of the eddying clouds within the crystal.

Vaguely the scene had a suggestion of familiarity to him, but even while he puzzled over it —half-amused, half-serious —the mist cleared again, and another picture formed beneath his gaze.

This time the distinct outline of a man's head and shoulders rose against the murky background of swirling clouds. Sexton Blake bent quizzical eyes upon the form represented. There was a queer familiarity about the set of those shoulders and the poise of that head. The picture grew in intensity. Suddenly Blake struck the table with his closed hand as —for one moment —the face showed forth with startling clearness. An exclamation escaped him.

Blake's ejaculation and the crash of his hand on the table drew a shuddering sigh from "Isolte," who appeared to wake from a species of trance, whether real or assumed, Blake could not tell. As a matter of fact, he was again smiling inwardly, when "Isolte's" voice came across the table with a hint of reproach in its tones.

"The signor is not ignorant of the occult sciences, but he is sceptical of the truths they teach."

Blake rose.

"I am afraid so, madame, with all due deference to your powers."

As he laid a couple of crisp notes on the table, Isolte placed her hand on his.

"Again I warn you! —Take heed!— Beware of the danger that lies in your path!"

The detective bowed courteously.

"I thank you, madame; I shall do all in my power to—" he laughed, "protect myself. Good-bye."

Once outside the tent, Blake immediately sought his hostess' side and made his adieux. As he turned away and strode across the green lawn towards the broad drive, where the "Grey Panther" stood, he was wholly unaware of the dismay in two pairs of eyes that watched his departure.

How little did Yvonne and Tinker realise, as they saw Blake climb into the car and a moment later drive away from their view, what terrible mental anxiety they both would be subjected to ere they set eyes on him again.

BLAKE was in a pre-occupied mood as he turned into the main road and guided the "Grey Panther" through the crowds of the curious who had gathered outside the gates to see what they could of the fashionable bazaar that was being held within.

Yvonne and Tinker, who had watched him depart, were mistaken in thinking that Blake's mind still dwelt on the incident that had taken place earlier in the afternoon. As a matter of fact, it had quite passed from his thoughts, for, despite his amused cynicism in "Isolte's" tent, what he had seen in the crystal had given him food for thought.

It was while he was striding towards the car that the vague familiarity of the first vision he had seen crystallised into a definite picture in which he himself had taken a. part. That picture, he now knew, had been an extraordinarily faithful replica of the scene at the shareholders' meeting of the Universal Machine Company a few days before.

While he was sceptical of anything of real value being obtained through the medium of such things as crystals and planchettes, Blake was fully aware that some remarkable things did occur at times through their use, and, indeed, he himself had at one time made a very close scientific study of the whole subject in order to discover just what possibilities it might hold for unbiased research.

But he also knew that it might be quite possible that "Isolte" knew he had been at the shareholders' meeting, and had in some way produced the vision by trickery. Yet he had to admit that it was rather curious, and, further, that the first vision should be followed by that of a man whom he had encountered much in the past, for the features of him whom he had seen in the swirling mist of the crystal had been of the man the world knew as Professor Butterfield, but whom Blake knew as Huxton Rymer.

Then, again, there was "Isolte's" reiterated warning of danger — danger that was near. Such a warning made Blake smile inwardly, for never a day, never a moment passed that he was not in danger of some sort, either from the numerous criminals whom he had run to earth in the past, or from sources that were interested in bringing his present activities to a close.

Not for a long time had Blake's mind worked so slowly as on this day. During the morning he had been worried and preoccupied over the case of the disappearance of Whidden Crane, for, though he had made the closest investigations since he had accepted the case, he had been unable to discover a single trace of the missing manager.

He had counted more than he had imagined on the arrangements he had made for the afternoon and evening with Yvonne, and when her regrets had reached him over the telephone, his mental fatigue had turned into sharp irritation and an unreasoning anger that she should break the appointment for any other man.

It was in this state of mind he had gone to the bazaar, and if he had been his usual cool and collected self, it is safe to say that the events which were even then shaping themselves would have had a very different outcome.

For Sexton Blake was heading straight into one of the very few blunders to be counted against the extraordinary list of successes of his long career.

The instrument chosen by the forces which were working against him was, in this instance, an old woman who started to hobble across the road about a hundred yards from the gates through which Blake had driven a few minutes before.

Now the Grey Panther was purring along gently, not making more than six or seven miles an hour, while Blake had complete control, and could bring the car to a stop in half its own length. He noticed the old woman when he was still some twenty yards from her, and, almost mechanically, turned the steering wheel a little in order to bring the Grey Panther to the left, and thus leave plenty of room for the old soul to continue her course.

At the rate she was going, and the rate the Grey Panther was moving, there would be, in the ordinary course of things, a good ten feet between them as the car passed. And this was what Blake counted on.

In fact, beyond the first turn of the wheel he gave the old woman scarcely another thought, but, suddenly, when he had almost reached the line of her course and in another moment would have passed, the hag lifted her head as though only now aware that the car was coming.

Blake had already sounded the syren twice, and now he pressed it again. Instead of going forward where it was quite clear, the old woman gave a screech and stumbled back towards the oncoming car.

With a sharp imprecation, Blake threw on the brakes, and the car stopped almost immediately. But, even as it did so, the old woman gave another loud cry and dropped to the road just beside the off front wheel.

Blake was out in a flash, and in two strides was bending over the moaning bundle which lay in the dust. Gently he placed his arms beneath her shoulders and lifted her up. As he did so her moans increased, but she allowed him to assist her to the car, where he opened the door of the tonneau and lifted her in.

"I am very, very sorry this has happened," he said soothingly. "Are you badly hurt?"

"Oh! Me leg, me leg!" moaned the hag.

"There," said Blake, patting her arm, "I think it is more fright than anything else. The car had really stopped when you struck it. But if you wish, I will take you to a hospital."

"No, not the 'ospital," she moaned.

"Then I will take you to your home," pursued Blake. "Is that what you wish?"

She mumbled an assent, and, after a few more efforts, Blake managed to elicit the address.

It proved to be what he knew was a most unsavoury quarter in the East End, and he was beginning to get irritated, as he had been anxious to return to Baker Street at once. Moreover, he was beginning to suspect that the old woman was exaggerating her mild injuries with the object of financial salve in view.

However, he realised there was nothing else for it, and, as a crowd was beginning to come along from the bazaar, he climbed back into his seat and started off once more. And while he was practically certain his passenger was, in the argot of certain quarters, "trying it on," it never occurred to him that the whole thing had been carefully planned, and had developed exactly as its authors had hoped.

On reaching Piccadilly Circus, Blake turned down the Haymarket and drove along Pall Mall until he came to Trafalgar Square. From there he went by way of Northumberland Avenue to the Embankment, where he let the Grey Panther out a little.

From time to time he turned his head to see how his passenger was getting on. She sat huddled up in one corner of the seat, emitting low moans at regular intervals, which Blake shrewdly guessed were for his especial benefit. At Blackfriars he drove by way of Queen Victoria Street to the Mansion House, and thence up Cornhill and on to Aldgate.

The address which the old woman had given him was, he knew, in Poplar, but not until he had driven through several unsavoury streets near the docks in that part of the East End did he discover that his destination was a very dirty corner "pub," above which there appeared to be three floors of tenement rooms. Blake drew up at the side entrance and got out.

"Is this the place?" he asked, as he opened the tonneau.

"Yes, the top floor. But oh! Me leg! Me leg! I never can walk it!"

"Have you anyone up there who can assist you?"

"Only me son, and 'e ain't at 'ome."

"Then I think I will have to carry you," remarked Blake cheerfully. "Come along, mother, you'll be all right in a few minutes, and I will give you some money before I leave."

Snuffling and moaning, the hag permitted Blake to gather her up and carry her across the footpath. Holding her thus he opened the door and stepped into the dirty and malodorous little hall from which a rickety flight of stairs led to the floor above.

Outside there had been few persons to witness their arrival, for it was still too early for the public-house to open, but, as he passed up the stairs, Blake saw several doors open surreptitiously then close swiftly as the old woman screamed a curse at the curious ones. It was evident to Blake that the old harridan was thoroughly feared by the other tenants.

Up the second flight of stairs Blake bore his burden, and there the old woman indicated a door straight before them as the one leading to her room. Blake turned the handle and pushed it open.

Before him he saw a dirty, littered kennel, in one corner of which was an old iron bed with a few filthy blankets heaped upon it. He carried his burden across, and bending over laid her on the bed. As he released her he thrust one hand into the pocket of his waistcoat and took out a roll of Treasury notes, which he placed in her greedy fingers.

Then he started to straighten up, and half turned as he heard a slight sound behind him. The next instant something descended on the back of his head with stunning force, and Blake sprawled forward across the old hag, who was now cackling with unholy glee.

Standing over the bed with arm upraised, ready to bring down the blackjack again should his victim show signs of consciousness, was the hulking figure of a ruffian whose features Blake would have recognised had he turned his head a moment sooner.

He would not have placed him as the son of the old hag who had acted as the instrument for his undoing, but as Thruster Joe, a survival of the old type of bludgeoning criminal with half a dozen records of Dartmoor behind him.

But, while the actual springing of the trap had been carried out by Thruster Joe and the old woman, it had never been conceived by the brute mentality of the ex-convict. It was the simple scheme of one who knew only too well the exact calibre of the finely attuned mental machine possessed by Sexton Blake, and who, in the very simplicity, almost primitive crudeness of the trap, had enticed his victim where a more elaborate and subtle scheme would have failed. And through the doorway now came he who had baited the trap —he whose features Sexton Blake had seen only an hour or so before in the mists of the crystal —Dr. Huxton Rymer.

Behind him there came another, whose presence would have been of extreme interest to Sexton Blake had he been conscious, for it was Whidden Crane, the absconding general manager of the Universal Machine Company. Of the two, it was plain that Rymer was the dominating force.

Pausing by the bed, he gazed down at the unconscious Blake. Then he made a sign to Thruster Joe.

"Take his heels," he ordered curtly.

The ex-convict obeyed, while Rymer got his hands under Blake's, shoulders. Preceded by Crane, they carried the unconscious man out of the room and along the passage to an adjoining kennel. There they dropped him on a bed as dirty as the one across which he had fallen, and, while Crane closed the door and started to take off his outer clothes, Rymer and Thruster Joe began to disrobe Blake.

When they had finished Rymer tossed the garments aside, and between them they managed to get Blake's relaxed body into Crane's clothes. That done, Rymer made another gesture, and, in obedience to the sign, Thruster Joe began to bind and gag Blake with a dexterity that had only been gained by long practice.

" I am going out for a few minutes, sir," said Mrs. Bardell. " Do you want me for anything before I go ? " The man at the table mumbled a reply under his breath. (*Chapter 4.*)

The Fourth Chapter. Rymer takes Charge —A Cunning Scheme —The Scout's Report —"All's Well" —The Descent on Baker Street —Getting Away with it.

MEANTIME, Rymer had crossed the room and taken up a small brown leather bag, which had been placed on the floor near a plain deal table. Seating himself, he opened the bag and began to lay several articles on the table. It was a curious array of small tubes and jars, and a few minutes later their purpose was obvious. But before going to work Rymer turned to survey the result of Thruster Joe's efforts. He nodded his head, then said:

"Blindfold him. Afterwards go through at once to Baker Street and keep watch. You will recognise the car. As soon as you see it, signal if the coast is clear. Do you understand?"

"I understand all right, boss."

"Then go. As soon as you have signalled return here. You know what you have to do then."

Thruster Joe tied a tight bandage over Blake's eyes, then took his departure, while Rymer set to work on Crane's features, talking in a low monotone as he worked.

"You are near enough his height and build," he said, as he rubbed a preliminary film of grease on the other's face; "but don't forget what I told you about carrying yourself straighter. You mustn't stoop as you naturally do. You ought to be able to get away with it all right, if the assistant goes out.

"It will be dusk, and you won't need more than five minutes or so in the place. And, above all, don't lose your nerve. There is a housekeeper there, a middle-aged woman. You will have to look out for her; but you ought not to find it difficult to slip past her. Besides, with his hat and clothes and motoring coat, you will look enough like him in the dusk. Your features are not the most difficult part. What I am worrying chiefly about is your walk. You mustn't forget that for a single moment."

Thus, while he worked, Rymer talked, until a slight movement on the part of the unconscious man on the bed caused him to desist. Then he went on in silence—lining here, smoothing there, and applying a slight artificial touch from time to time, until he had altered Crane's features into a fair resemblance to those of Blake. When he had finished he signed to Crane.

20

The two men rose, and Rymer assisted the other into Blake's long motoring coat. He spent some minutes getting the exact angle for the grey soft hat that Blake had worn; then he stepped back, and gave a close scrutiny to the result.

At last he nodded his head with satisfaction.

Quietly they made for the door, and slipped out into the hall. Rymer closed the door, and led the way along to another room, which was a trifle cleaner than the two they had already been in. When the door had been closed he pulled out his cigarette-case.

"You will have time for a cigarette before you go," he said. "We will have to give Thruster Joe time to do his scouting. Now let us go over the keys you have in your pocket. I fancy we will be able to pick out the ones you may find useful."

Crane drew out Blake's bunch of keys, and, taking them in his hand. Rymer studied them one by one.

"This, I fancy, will be the key of the front door," he said, indicating a small one; "and one of these two ought to fit his desk. Of course, I don't know where you will find what you want, but I should certainly have a go at the desk first. Now, don't forget the plan of the place as I have described it. I have no reason to believe that there has been any interior alteration since I was there some years ago. And, again, remember you must work quickly. Don't try to gather too much. A little will do, just to complete the impression we want to give."

"I will remember," replied Crane. "You needn't fear that I will stay any longer than I have to. I will go for the passport first, and after that get a bag and some clothes out of the dressing-room. There is no danger of my losing my nerve now. I have too much at stake."

"You have your liberty at stake," rejoined Rymer coolly. "If you bungle this it is going to be very difficult to get you out of England. You can take it that every port land railway-station is being watched closely. A week ago we might have figured out something else. But now that the police are on the job, and since the Universal has put the matter in Blake's hands, it is too late to try a forged passport.

"But if you keep your nerve, and with some luck, we will hoodwink them yet. And it will be a long time before we have anything to fear from him."

With these words Rymer jerked his head in the direction of the room where the unconscious Blake lay.

They smoked in silence for another quarter of an hour. Then Rymer tossed his cigarette away and rose.

"You had better start now," he said. "I will wait here."

Crane got to his feet and started for the door. He passed out into the hall and down the rickety stairs to the street. There he found a few idlers gathered about the Grey Panther, for it was not often that a car of that type was seen in these surroundings.

Crane thrust one of the loiterers aside and climbed in. He was a little nervous of the start, for it was only that day that he had had a first lesson in the handling of the particular make of car which Rymer had ascertained that Blake drove. But his hand was steady enough as he pressed the self-starter, and a moment later the car drew away smoothly.

Crane took things easy for some distance, but by the time he had reached Aldgate he had gained more confidence. It was still light, and, as he wanted to arrive at Baker Street as near dusk as possible, he drove leisurely until he reached Oxford Street. There he turned into Orchard Street, and drew into the kerb.

As he did so. a man who had been strolling along the street paused by the car, and said in low, hurried tones:

"Green telephones that the assistant has just left the garden-party in a two-seater driven by a girl. Joe is round the corner."

Crane nodded, and drove on slowly until he came to the corner of Baker Street. As he turned into the street, Thruster Joe came towards him, and gave a signal which had been arranged on. At that Crane drove along, and brought the car to a stop just outside Blake's house.

He climbed out, and, leaving the engine running, crossed the footpath to the steps. He drew out his keys, and selected the one which Rymer had opined might fit the front door. Rymer's judgment proved right, for, with little difficulty, Crane got the key in and turned.

As he stepped into the hall his heart quickened, for he knew just what discovery would mean. He pulled himself together, however, and, recalling what Rymer had told him about the arrangement of the house, climbed the stairs until he came to what he thought must be the door of the consulting-room. He hesitated for a second, with his fingers on the handle, then turned and entered. He knew at the first glance that he had not been mistaken.

Swiftly his eyes went towards the desk.

Crossing the room, he seated himself, and chose one of the smaller keys. Then, after pulling open the two top drawers, which were unlocked, he tried the key. It was necessary to fit it into three of the drawers before he was able to turn it. A very brief examination of the contents of the compartment showed him that what he sought was not there. He chose another key, and persisted in his efforts. Two more drawers he opened without success. Then he managed to get the lowest drawer on the right to open, and as he turned over the contents he suddenly saw what he wanted. He took it up and opened it, to make sure that it was current and not out of date.

Not only was it Blake's current passport, but on the back Crane saw the especial police visa that covered at once every country with which Britain was on terms of extradition.

In that moment Whidden Crane felt a deep respect for the mind of Dr. Huxton Rymer, the man on whom all his hopes now hung.

He closed the drawer swiftly, and, still adhering to Rymer's instructions, crossed the consulting-room to a second door that led to the passage which served the laboratory and the bed-rooms and dressing-rooms on that floor. He found a dressing-room, which a brief examination showed him was Blake's.

Now he worked swiftly. First he selected a medium-sized crocodile suitcase from a pile in the corner. Opening it, he then took from one of the wardrobes one of Blake's suits, an overcoat, a pair of shoes; some socks and shirts and ties from a big chest of drawers, and a motoring-cap from the array which hung on the wall.

Piling these into the suitcase, he closed it with a snap. Then suddenly his heart went into his mouth as there came a rap on the door. Keeping his face averted, he gave an exclamation. The door opened, and the next instant he heard a voice which he knew must be that of Blake's housekeeper.

"I am going out for a few minutes, sir," she said. "Do you want me for anything before I go?"

Crane mumbled something which he meant for a negative; then held himself tense as he waited to see if the woman suspected anything.

But apparently Mrs. Bardell never dreamed for a moment that it was not Blake to whom she had been speaking, for she closed the door, and Crane breathed easier as he heard her retreating along the passage. He waited a few moments longer; then, picking up the suitcase, made his way back.

Just as he reached it he heard the front door slam, and, hurrying to the window, saw Mrs. Bardell go down the steps and along the street. Crane stepped stealthily out into the hall and made for the front door. For a moment he hesitated to take the plunge into the street; but, with Rymer's warning in his mind, he opened the door and stepped out. He hurried down the steps and to the car.

Tossing the suitcase into the back, he climbed in and took the wheel. Even as he did so he caught a glimpse of a two-seater just swinging into Baker Street. In it was a girl and a young man, and Whidden Crane did not need much deduction to guess that it was Tinker.

He threw in the clutch, and sent the Grey Panther ahead with a jerk. He swung round the first corner, and drove at reckless speed for Oxford Street; while, behind him, Tinker and Yvonne, seated in the two-seater which Yvonne had brought to a stop at the kerb in front of the house, pondered on the extraordinary vagaries which Sexton Blake had exhibited that day.

And the morning papers for the next day announced briefly that "Mr. Sexton Blake, the well-known criminologist, had left for the Continent."

*The Fifth Chapter.   No News is Bad News —The Lost Steel
Formula —Tinker is Distracted —Has Blake Gone to America? —
The Wireless Question.*

"CAN you understand it, mademoiselle? I can't. Such a thing has never happened before, and it isn't a bit like the guv'nor. Even if he were deeply annoyed about something, he wouldn't go off in such a way and leave so many important things unattended to. I can't help but think that there is something wrong somewhere."

Mademoiselle Yvonne dropped the ashes from the end of the cigarette she was smoking, and gazed thoughtfully at Tinker, who had come round to her offices in Oxford Street to unburden his mind of the worry that had been racking him for three days.

It was a little over that length of time since Sexton Blake had apparently taken an unceremonious departure from Baker Street. At first, Tinker had thought little about the absence of his chief, for he knew it had been Blake's intention to run across to the Continent for a day or so to dispose of a matter which the Prefect of Police of Paris was holding up for his arrival.

As usual, during periods of Blake's absence, Tinker had dealt with routine affairs, although several matters had come up which needed his master's personal attention and signature. For two days Tinker had carried on as best he could, but when, on the third day, there was still no word from Blake, the lad had taken the liberty of getting through on the telephone to the Prefect in Paris.

What that gentleman had said had amazed Tinker. He had neither seen nor heard anything of Blake, but had been expecting his arrival in Paris for some days. Tinker had not committed himself to any definite statement, but had simply thanked the prefect, and hung up the receiver. Shortly after that, however, this very morning, in fact, an incident had occurred that had determined him to talk things over with Yvonne.

That was the visit of Sir Frederick Cameron, chairman of the board of directors of the Universal Machine Company.

The baronet had arrived in an extremely agitated state of mind, and had appeared distinctly upset when informed by Tinker that Blake was still out of town.

After some indecision he had confided in Tinker the reason for wishing to consult with Blake urgently, and Tinker, who had known that Blake was working on the disappearance of Whidden Crane with £150,000 of the firm's funds, had realised that what Sir Frederick had told him was a very serious factor, of which Blake ought to be informed without delay.

He had again committed himself to nothing definite, but had promised the anxious baronet that he would communicate the new information to Blake at the earliest possible moment. With that Sir Frederick had departed, and a few minutes later Tinker had gone round to see Yvonne.

"I certainly agree with you, Tinker, that it is extremely unlike Mr. Blake to act in this way, and particularly to allow matters of importance to pile up with out keeping you advised how you should deal with them. But what can we do? We both saw him drive away from Baker Street, and he must have seen us, for he turned round. If he had wished to give you any instructions he could have done so then."

"I know, but since then some things have come up that he couldn't foresee. One thing this morning is awfully important, and the guv'nor must be told about it soon."

"Do you care to confide in me?"

"Well, that is really what I came round for. I will tell you what it is. A few days ago the guv'nor took up a case for the Universal Machine Company. You probably read in the papers that Whidden Crane, the general manager of the company absconded with a big bunch of money."

"Yes, I read that. The papers said the amount was in the neighbourhood of £150,000."

"That's right. The company got into financial difficulties over the affair, and a meeting of the shareholders was called. The guv'nor had some shares, so went along to the meeting. It was after that that someone suggested that he should try and locate Crane. The guv'nor accepted, and we have been making inquiries since, but without any success so far.

"Well, this morning Sir Frederick Cameron, the chairman of the company, came to see the guv'nor. He was very upset when I told him he was still out of town. He then told me the reason for his visit, and that is what the guv'nor must be told."

"What was the reason, Tinker?"

"This is very confidential, mademoiselle. It seems that, during the course of further investigations at the offices of the company, it was discovered yesterday afternoon that a secret formula of great value had been taken from the vaults. This formula is of a secret process for the manufacture of a metal known as 'white steel.' From what Sir Frederick told me, it is a metal as light as aluminium, but with the strength of the finest vanadium steel, and would revolutionise the design of aeroplane and aircraft engines.

"He said that they had been carrying out secret experiments with great success, and that it had been the intention of the company to manufacture for the British Government on a royalty basis. He thinks Crane must have taken it with the intention of trying to sell it to some foreign Power. It looks as though he is right, because only he, the secretary of the company, and Crane knew where the formula was kept."

"That is certainly serious," remarked Yvonne. "What steps have you taken to try and get in touch with Mr. Blake?"

"I telephoned to the prefect in Paris, but he had not seen or heard anything, although he had been expecting the guv'nor to call on him. That was his reason for going across to the Continent."

Suddenly Yvonne bent an uneasy gaze upon the lad.

"Do you think it possible that something has happened to him?" she asked, in anxious tones.

"I have thought of that as well. Of course, there are a lot of people who would do the guv'nor in —and me, too, for the matter of that —if they got the chance. But he usually manages to take care of himself. Besides, I looked into things at Baker Street. He certainly did not intend staying away long, for he only took one suitcase with him. That and his passport seem to be about all he had."

"And yet you have heard absolutely nothing from him?"

"Not a word. That is what worries me. There are some matters that he certainly should have given me instructions about, and other things have come up since he left. Of course, I can always sign for him under the special power of attorney I hold, but I only make use of that in emergencies."

"If he went across to the Continent it should not be difficult to locate him if nothing has happened. He is so well known, and I presume he was travelling under his own name?"

"As far as I know, yes. And he went across the Channel all right. I know that, because it appears he drove the car to Charing Cross.

There he got hold of a taxi man, who drove the Grey Panther back to the garage for him. He told them at the garage that Mr. Blake had sent the car back, as he was going out of town."

"That was not like him," remarked Yvonne quickly.

"No, I agree with you. Ordinarily, when I am not at hand to drive him to the station, he takes a taxi."

"There is something about it that I don't like—" began Yvonne, but broke off as a tap came at the door. It opened to reveal the genial and immaculately-clad Graves. He nodded to Yvonne, and, turning to Tinker, said:

"Hallo, Tinker! How goes the strenuous pursuit of the wily dodger in the absence of the chief?"

Tinker grinned.

"Not so well," he replied. "We were just talking about him."

"Not an unusual topic of conversation when you and Yvonne get together," rejoined Graves, while Yvonne changed colour. "But what has started him off to America this time?"

"America!" exclaimed Tinker and Yvonne in one breath. "What do you mean?"

"Just what I say," responded Graves, gazing at them in surprise. "What do you mean?"

"But —but America," stammered Tinker. "I don't understand."

"Do you mean to say you didn't know he had gone?" queried the amazed Graves.

"Yes. How did you know, Mr. Graves?"

"Why, I saw his name in the list of passengers in a paper at the club. I was amused, because in the same list is the name of an old friend of Blake. I wondered if Blake was after him again."

"Who is that?" asked Tinker quickly.

"Well, he is down as Professor Butterfield, but I have strong suspicions that it is none other than Huxton Rymer."

"What steamer was it?"

"The French liner Orleans. She sailed from Havre four days or so ago."

Tinker and Yvonne exchanged quick glances. It was Yvonne who spoke first.

"That would be it," she said. "She must have sailed the morning after he left for the Continent. It certainly seems very strange that he would leave for New York without a word to you, Tinker."

"Not only strange, but a thing he has never in his life done before," muttered Tinker, with a suspicious quiver in his voice as he thought that it could only mean Blake was deeply displeased with him over something.

Graves was studying the pair of them with questioning eyes.

"Do I understand that Blake has gone off on a jaunt to New York without a word to Tinker?"

Yvonne nodded.

"It appears so. Do you think you could have been mistaken, uncle?"

"Not a chance. I noticed it particularly, because I was amused to see that he was on the same ship with his old enemy."

Tinker rose.

"I am going back to Baker Street," he said heavily.

Yvonne jumped up and laid a hand on his shoulder.

"What are you going to do, Tinker?"

"I don't know exactly. But one thing I shall try. I shall put through a wireless message. If I can't reach the ship direct, I may be able to get it relayed by some other steamer. The Orleans is very fast. She must be two-thirds of the way across by now."

"Yes I should certainly do that," agreed Yvonne decisively. "And please let me know the moment you hear anything, Tinker."

Tinker nodded, and turned towards the door, while Yvonne watched him with sympathy and understanding.

As Tinker made his way back to Baker Street his mind was in a chaos of doubt and indecision.

"I can't understand it!" he muttered over and over again. "To think of the guv'nor going off like that without a word. Hang it! Even if he was sore at me about something, it isn't like him to leave affairs in the state they are. They have got to be attended to, and if he can't do it, I must. Anyway, I will try and get in touch with him and ask him what I am to do."

With that decision he quickened his pace. Back in the consulting-room, he drew a form from the pile on the desk, and began to write a message. When he had finished he had achieved this:

"Sexton Blake, passenger on board ss. Orleans,—Please advise me urgently what I must do regarding matters here. Several need immediate attention. Further information vital importance regarding recent case, has reached me. Advise fully.—TINKER."

Stuffing the message in his pocket, Tinker left the house, and made his way to the garage. Climbing into the Grey Panther, he drove to Cockspur Street to the London offices of the French line to which the Orleans belonged.

There he inspected a copy of the passengers who had sailed by that ship, and came upon Blake's name, just as Graves had told him. He also saw the name of Professor Butterfield.

It did not give the first name of the professor, but, as Tinker did not know of any other Professor Butterfield than Rymer, he was inclined to agree with Graves.

Could it be possible, he asked himself, that Blake had come on some sudden clue in one of the cases he was investigating that had caused him to dash across to Havre and catch the Orleans? And might this clue have had something to do with Huxton Rymer?

On reflection, he decided it did not seem reasonable, for there was still the mystery as to why Blake had not sent him a single word.

Tinker next sent in his name to the manager of the passenger department, and to that gentleman explained his reasons for calling. It occurred to Tinker that the agents for the line would probably be able to get into direct communication with the ship sooner than he would be able to do so through ordinary channels. His plan proved wise, for the manager said:

"We are not keen on doing this sort of thing, but, considering the identity of the passenger, I shall be glad to assist you. I doubt if we shall be able to reach the Orleans direct, but her sister ship, the Tours, is on her way across and is only two days out now. We can get her to relay the message to the Orleans."

Tinker thanked him, and with the assurance that the message would be got away without delay, drove back to Baker Street. There he telephoned to Yvonne, telling her what he had done. After that he had a hurried lunch, then settled down to a long afternoon's grind at the work that had piled up since Blake's departure.

The Sixth Chapter. The Wireless Reply —Yvonne on the Right Track —Mrs. Bardell is Cross-examined —Tinker Investigated —A Cable from the States.

FIVE o'clock had just struck when the telephone-bell rang. Tinker found that it was the manager of the passenger department who had sent his message for him.

"We have a reply," he said. "Shall I send it on to you, or will you call in for it?"

"I'll come along there at once," replied Tinker.

With that, he hung up the receiver, and, grabbing his cap, hurried out to the car, which he had left standing at the kerb. He drove at reckless speed to Cockspur Street, and dashed into the steamship company's office like a whirlwind.

He paused only long enough to thank the manager for his courtesy, then returned to the car, where he tore open the envelope of the wireless message. But as he read the contents he gave a quick frown, for, instead of settling the problems that were puzzling him, they only deepened his perplexity.

The message read thus:

"Carry on until my return. Accept no new business, and suspend all action in cases pending. Date of my return uncertain, but will advise you.—SEXTON BLAKE."

Tinker folded up the message thoughtfully, and stuffed it into his pocket. He climbed slowly into the car, and headed for Oxford Street. He wanted to see Yvonne, and show her the strange communication he had received from Blake. But on arriving at her offices found that she had left. He then drove on to the flat at Queen Anne's Gate.

Yvonne was in the smoking-room at the end of the hall, writing. She glanced up with a look of inquiry as the lad entered, and held out the message. Yvonne took it eagerly, but as she read the contents, frowned, as had Tinker. Yvonne let her hands drop and gazed at the lad.

"What do you make of it, Tinker?"

"I don't know what to say, mademoiselle. It has absolutely flabbergasted me. First, the guv'nor goes off without saying a word to me. Then he leaves me without any instructions as to how I am to carry on. On top of that, when he does reply to my wireless, he tells me to carry on as best I can, and to suspend all action in current cases.

"That is what puzzles me more than anything. It isn't like the guv'nor to take up a case, and then drop it."

"Do you know what I think, Tinker?"

"What is that?"

"I do not believe that this message was ever sent by Mr. Blake."

"Not sent by the guv'nor!" exclaimed Tinker. "What do you mean?"

"Exactly what I say. I have had an uneasy feeling ever since our conversation this morning. I can't explain why, but my instinct tells me that there is something wrong somewhere."

"But I sent the wireless to the Orleans, and the guv'nor answered it."

"Quite so. But how do we know that it is Mr. Blake who is on the Orleans? Listen, Tinker! Let us just look at the events of the past few days. In no single instance, from the moment we saw Mr. Blake drive away from the bazaar, has he acted as we, who know him so well, would expect him to act.

"Granted that he may have been irritated and annoyed on that afternoon, he would never allow such a state of mind to interfere with his work. Nor would he dash off to New York without advising you fully how you were to carry on. He had that opportunity when he drove away from Baker Street —if it was he whom we saw."

"Good heavens! Mademoiselle, what do you mean?"

"I don't know exactly. But, Tinker, did that person act as Mr. Blake would have acted? Could anyone, as scrupulous about his engagements as Mr. Blake, leave his affairs in this muddle, and calmly wave his responsibilities aside as the sender of this message has done?"

"No, it doesn't seem like the guv'nor."

"It is only instinct on my part, Tinker, but they say that a woman's instinct is sometimes more to be trusted than cold logic. Then, again, I see a very suspicious circumstance in the presence on board of Dr. Huxton Rymer."

"Do you mean that you think someone on the Orleans is masquerading as the guv'nor?"

"I am not prepared to go that far, but I certainly think it entirely possible. Wouldn't that explain a great deal that has been puzzling us?"

"Then where is the guv'nor?" cried Tinker.

Yvonne plainly reflected the lad's uneasiness.

"That is what we have got to set ourselves to find out, Tinker," she said slowly. "If my instinct is right, then— then something may have happened to him days ago, and he may need our assistance desperately." And her voice broke as the thought of a worse possibility rose up before her.

"In that case, then, the man we saw drive away from Baker Street in the Grey Panther was not the guv'nor," said Tinker soberly. "And —Good heavens, if that is so, then something must have happened to the guv'nor after he left the bazaar!"

"Yes," cried Yvonne excitedly. "And don't you see what else, Tinker? That man who was masquerading as Mr. Blake may have gone to Baker Street just to get Mr. Blake's passport."

"If it wasn't the guv'nor, then they must have trapped him just before that!" muttered Tinker. "Anyway, the man we saw was certainly wearing the guv'nor's motoring coat and hat, and I could have sworn that it was he."

"It was dusk, and we could not see very plainly."

"I know. Anyway, I must look into things at Baker Street at once. If you are right, then the trail starts there; but I can't see where it will lead to."

"We can also get a cable away at once to Bryant Kennedy —Mr. Blake's New York correspondent. We can ask him to meet the Orleans on her arrival, and find out the truth."

Tinker nodded.

"I will get one away at once. Then I will go on to Baker Street, and try to get a line on something there."

Yvonne went with him to the front door. Just before he opened it she clasped her hands about his arm.

"Keep in touch with me, Tinker!" she pleaded. "I —I shall worry horribly until we know the truth."

Tinker shyly laid his hand on the gleaming coils of her lovely hair.

"You know I will do that," he said gruffly, and with that he was gone.

Tinker's first duty was to get an urgent cable away to Bryant Kennedy. Then he drove to Baker Street. On entering the consulting-room he rang for Mrs. Bardell. When the housekeeper had put in an appearance Tinker said:

"Mrs. Bardell, did you see the guv'nor the day he went away?"

"Why, yes, Master Tinker. He was in his dressing-room."

"I want you to think carefully, and tell me every detail you can remember."

The good soul wrinkled up her nose and thought hard for a few minutes. Then she said:

"Well, now as I come to think of it, there isn't much to tell. I was down in the basement when I heard him come in. I could hear him pulling out and shutting the drawers of the desk here, so I didn't disturb him. Then I heard him go along to his dressing-room. I was going out, and asked him if he wished anything before I went. He said he didn't. That is all, Master Tinker."

"Now, think again, Mrs. Bardell. Did you see him plainly? I mean, did you see his face?"

"I can't say as I did, Master Tinker. He was packing his suitcase, and didn't turn round."

"Ah! All right; that is all I wanted to know."

"Is anything wrong, Master Tinker?" asked the good soul anxiously.

"There is nothing for you to worry about," said Tinker. "Now let me think."

As soon as Mrs. Bardell had gone Tinker drew out his keys and seated himself at Blake's desk.

On his key-ring were duplicates of all the keys which Blake carried.

Swiftly Tinker began an examination of the drawers. With the exception of a cursory glance into the one where Blake had kept his passport he had not looked into the others since his master's departure. Now he went at his work slowly and methodically, and by the time he had reached the last one his young eyes were clouded with deep worry.

When he had finished he hurried along to Blake's dressing-room, and there began to make a minute inventory of the contents of the wardrobes and chests of drawers. It took him well over an hour, so methodical was he; but when he had finished the expression in his eyes had not changed.

Back in the consulting-room once more, he seated himself at the desk, and drew the telephone instrument towards him. A few moments later he heard Yvonne's voice at the other end of the wire.

"I am beginning to think there is something in what you suggest, mademoiselle," he said quickly. "After sending the cable to Kennedy I came on here and began an investigation. I will tell you what I have been able to discover.

"Firstly. I questioned Mrs. Bardell. She saw the guv'nor just before he left. He was in his dressing room packing, but she remembers that when she spoke to him he didn't look round. Therefore, she didn't see his face. That is item one.

"Next, I tackled the desk, and went through every drawer systematically. I am certain that the contents of some of them have been turned over by someone not familiar with them, for two of them were in a state of confusion such as neither I nor the guv'nor would leave them. That might have been done by someone who was looking for the guv'nor's passport, and didn't know just where to find it."

"Yes, yes!" came Yvonne's voice excitedly. "What else, Tinker?"

"I next went into his dressing-room. I know pretty well what the guv'nor would take away with him on any journey, whether a long one or a short one. Well, from what I can discover, he seems to have made a queer selection. A suit is gone and a cap, but I can only find that he has taken one pair of socks, one shirt, and no pyjamas. Does that seem like the guv'nor?"

"It certainly seems an odd way to travel."

"That is all I have been able to discover so far," went on Tinker. "I can't see that we can do much more until we hear from Kennedy. I figure the Orleans will reach New York in another two days or two days and a half. So we should hear very soon after she has docked."

"You can only carry on until then, Tinker. But to-morrow we must make further efforts to trace his movements after he left the bazaar."

They arranged a rendezvous for the following morning, and when he had hung up the receiver Tinker settled down once more to work.

Neither Yvonne nor Tinker confessed to each other what they were feeling during the next two days.

Each was working desperately to try and find some clue to Blake's movements after he had driven away from the bazaar. But all to no purpose. By the end of the second day Tinker was in a state of acute nerves, and remained at Baker Street all day waiting for a reply from Kennedy. By inquiries at the offices of the French line he calculated that it would be possible to receive a cable by four o'clock in the afternoon, and from that on as the hours sped by with no word he grew more and more depressed.

Yvonne was on the 'phone every few minutes, asking for news which Tinker was unable to give her. At midnight he gave it up and turned in, trying to get some sleep. But he tossed restlessly all night, and was up again at daybreak. Not until ten o'clock did the anxiously looked-for message come. As Mrs. Bardell handed him the envelope Tinker tore it open, and with shaking fingers unfolded the form. As he read the contents he gave a sharp exclamation of disappointment, for Kennedy had wired:

"Regret only received your cable on my return from Washington four hours after Orleans docked. Am trying to trace Blake. Will telegraph immediately I locate him.   KENNEDY."

Tinker laid the cable on the desk and reached for the telephone instrument, in order to communicate to Yvonne what Kennedy had said. He paused as the door of the consulting-room opened, then, with a cry, he bounded to his feet as through the doorway came Sexton Blake himself.

Thruster Joe and his helpless charge waited behind the shelter of a wall while the Greek skipper conversed in his broken English with the dock policeman. *(Chapter 7.)*

The Seventh Chapter.   What Happened to Sexton Blake —Thruster Joe gets a Temporary Revenge —Shanghaied —In the Greek Tramp's Hold —A Slender Chance of Escape.

TO understand how it was that Sexton Blake, thin and haggard and worn, walked into the consulting-room so dramatically after his mysterious absence of the past eight days, it is necessary to go back to the events which immediately followed the springing of the trap in the East End of London.

It is already known how successfully Rymer had been able to carry out his plans once he had disposed of Blake, and that the criminal adventurer was determined that Blake's enforced retirement from the scene should last for a considerable time was evident from the elaborate steps he took to ensure it.

When Crane had managed to bring off his coup at Baker Street, and secure Blake's passport, he had driven the Grey Panther to Charing Cross, and there, as Tinker had discovered by inquiries at the garage, had hired a taximan to drive the car back to the garage, taking pains to let him know that it had been sent by Sexton Blake.

As soon as the man had driven off, Crane, instead of entering the station, had passed out of the courtyard, and had hailed a taxi in the Strand. From there he had driven through to the tenement in Poplar, where Rymer was waiting.

The two choice rogues had lain low there until it was time to leave for Victoria, where they caught the boat train for Southampton. They had crossed to Havre, where, through the very daring of Rymer's plan, they had been able to pass on board the Orleans without question, and the following morning the liner had sailed for New York.

Rymer would have found it much easier to get away alone, but it did not suit his plans to separate from Crane just then.

It would have been of considerable interest to the directors of the Universal Machine Company to know that the huge defalcations of their general manager and the abstraction of the secret formula for the manufacture of "white steel" had been planned by, and executed under, the cunning direction of the well-known scientist, Professor Andrew Butterfield.

And Crane would have been equally perturbed if he had dreamed for a single moment that, instead of being contented with half which he hoped to receive for the formula through sources which will presently become apparent, and no part of the £150,000 which he had embezzled, Rymer had coolly decided that, when the right moment came, both the loot and the proceeds of the sale of the formula should go only into the capacious pockets of Dr. Huxton Rymer.

When that time should come he would find little difficulty in disposing of Crane. But not yet was the moment to spring his little surprise on the man who had proved such an apt tool for his purposes.

Once they were safely aboard the Orleans it was easy enough to avoid mixing with the other passengers by professing illness and remaining in their cabin, and, as a matter of fact, the only incident that occurred during the voyage was the startling message from Tinker that come out of the ether.

That had been a complication which Rymer had overlooked, but how he met it is already known.

In the meantime, back in the East End of London, Thruster Joe, the exconvict, was carrying out Rymer's instructions to the letter. The gaolbird found a peculiar pleasure in his duties, for he had a long-standing grudge against Sexton Blake.

Not only had Blake been the cause of Thruster Joe spending some three years as an unwilling guest in one of those places which are so easy to get into but so hard to get out of, but Blake had also upset a very profitable bit of work not long before, just at the moment when Thruster Joe was about to collect.[1]

Moreover, Rymer had paid him well, and Thruster Joe was determined on doing one of the most conscientious jobs of his career.

Blake was kept a prisoner in the tenement until late that night, but Thruster Joe himself departed shortly after dusk. His objective was a small Greek steamer which lay in the docks less than a hundred yards from the saloon.

In the cabin of the dingy tramp Thruster Joe had a long and earnest conversation with the dirty and garlic-scented Greek skipper. Then the two had left the steamer and had walked along to the saloon, where they imbibed freely until closing time.

Their next action was to mount to the top floor of the tenement, where they sat waiting until the loafers had cleared away from the

---

[1] This was the time when Blake assisted Mademoiselle Yvonne in her first case —see "U.J." No 963, The Affair of the Patagonian Devil.

corner beneath. Following this, the pair entered the room where Sexton Blake lay. Blake had regained consciousness, and had turned over on his side, so that his eyes could watch the door. As he saw Thruster Joe enter, bearing a small oil lamp, Blake realised only too plainly the nature of the trap he had walked into. Thruster Joe lurched across and stared down at him.

"How do you feel now, Mr. Sexton Blake?" he jeered. "Things are a little different since last we met. Then it was me what was down and you what was doin' the laugh. I told you I'd get you one day, and now I have you just where I want you. And you're going for a nice little journey where you'll be out of the way for some time!"

Blake's gag made it impossible for him to reply, but as the ex-convict jeered, a sardonic expression came into Blake's eyes which maddened Thruster Joe. Lifting his free hand, he brought it down heavily across Blake's eyes, and would have repeated the blow had not the Greek captain restrained him.

"You make da noise!" he snarled. "Com', we getta da stiff away!"

With a curse, Thruster Joe set the lamp down and caught hold of Blake's shoulders. The Greek took his heels, and in this way they carried him through the door to the hall.

The old hag put in an appearance then, and, grabbing the lamp, held it to light their way down the rickety stairs. Once in the street, they hurried along until they had reached the high wall which enclosed the docks.

There was one moment of danger to their plan, for if the guard was on duty at the gate there would be questions asked, and no lies could explain why their burden was bound and gagged.

But the Greek and Thruster Joe knew every inch of the place, and just before they came to the danger spot they laid their burden down while the Greek went ahead. Thruster Joe, who waited, heard him in conversation with the dock policeman; then their voices died away as they crossed to the edge of the basin where the Greek captain had lured the policeman on a trumped-up complaint.

That was Thruster Joe's moment, and he wasted no time in seizing it.

Sexton Blake was a heavy man, but Thruster Joe was equal to the task. He picked Blake up bodily, and, with his burden hanging loosely over his shoulders, stole along and whipped through the gate like a shadow. He kept on in the direction of the small Greek steamer until he came to a pile of scantlings.

Behind these he dumped his burden, and made along to where the Greek was talking unintelligible English to the bewildered and irritated constable. The constable knew Thruster Joe as a casual dock labourer, and when he went off to the Greek steamer with the dirty captain he thought nothing of it. On the contrary, he was relieved to get rid of the foreigner.

Thruster Joe and the Greek had little difficulty in transporting their burden the remaining distance, and ten minutes later Sexton Blake was lying on a pile of cases in the forward hold of the tramp.

Before parting, Thruster Joe and the Greek disposed of a further quantity of raw spirit in the cabin. Then the exconvict lurched away, well satisfied with the result of his night's work, and the richer by two hundred pounds in crisp notes

Sexton Blake's head was still groggy from the effects of the heavy blow Thruster Joe had dealt him, and for some hours after being thrown into the forward hold like a sack of wheat he lay in a half-doze, scarcely conscious of his surroundings. He had got one glimpse by lantern light of the interior of the hold, and had guessed that he was being shanghaied out of the country. But not until the jerky throb of the screw roused him from his lethargy did he realise that morning must have arrived, and that they were probably on their way down the Thames.

It was hours later before one of the hatch boards was removed, allowing daylight to penetrate into the hold. Through the opening came a deck hand of a type in keeping with the skipper of the dirty craft. In one hand he carried a bucket which proved to contain a mess of soup and meat.

Blake's nostrils twitched as the odour reached him, for his throat was dry and swollen from the gag, and it was nearly twenty-four hours since he had had either food or drink.

The deck hand untied the bandage and removed the gag, after which he held up the bucket to Blake's mouth. Blake eagerly sucked at the unsavoury liquid, but, hungry though he was refused the chunks of meat which the deck hand tried to thrust into his mouth. He did not persist, for it was a matter of the utmost indifference to him whether the prisoner took the food or not.

Like every other hand on board, he had been given to understand by the captain that the prisoner was one who had assisted the Turks, the deadly enemies of the Greeks, against their own country, and that he was being taken to Greece, where vengeance would be wreaked on him.

Blake made an attempt to get the deck hand to talk, but his efforts were useless. For one thing he was glad, and that was that no attempt was made to replace the gag. He reasoned that the captain was far enough on his way to the Channel to feel safe, and, in fact, this was the case.

When the deck hand had departed, the hatch board was jammed back into place, and again Blake lay in the dark, the long hours dragging by on leaden feet. Some time in the night he was given another ration of the stew, and then again was left until the following day.

Now, during the hours which he had for contemplation, Blake had been pondering on the events that had led to his present predicament. While Thruster Joe had been the instrument of his undoing, Blake knew perfectly well that the scheme had not originated with the ex-convict.

In the first place, such a shanghaiing could only be carried out by the liberal use of money; and, secondly, Thruster Joe would not take such a line of revenge as that. His idea of getting even with Blake would be to bludgeon him to death.

Therefore Blake reasoned that there must be an influence behind Thruster Joe and the Greek captain which commanded plenty of money, and which had evolved a plot that was quite beyond the mental capacity of either of the other two.

Slowly and methodically Blake pieced together the few incidents of which he was cognisant, working back from the saloon in the East End to the moment when he had left the bazaar.

His senses had not left him under the blow from Thruster Joe's blackjack before he had heard the fiendish cackle of the old hag whom he had brought to the tenement, and, in that brief instant, it had flashed into Blake's mind that the whole thing had been a deliberately planned trap.

But who had laid it?

That was the question he kept asking himself over and over again. And as his thoughts probed back and back, searching and examining, it was inevitable that, under the lens of his seeking should come even trivial incidents of that afternoon.

He recalled, among other things, his visit to the tent of Isolte, the psychist, when he had turned into the first place at hand to avoid joining Yvonne and Tinker. He recalled her warning, and the trickery of the visions which he had seen in the crystal.

At the time he had been slightly amused, but mostly bored, even though the pictures themselves had been of subjects which had certainly touched his own life. But was it only trickery after all was it possible that some reflex of his own mind had caused him to visualise those things?

On his way to the Grey Panther he had recognised the first vision as a remarkable production of the shareholders' meeting in the board-room of the Universal Machine Company. And the second had certainly been the bearded countenance of Dr. Huxton Rymer.

Could it be possible that the apparent trance of the psychist had not been faked but had been an actual condition of subconscious dominance? Could it be that, in some psychic manner, she had felt the menace of threatening danger?

Isolte had reproached him for his scepticism, but, even so, she had repeated her warning earnestly, and it was certainly a fact that the danger had been imminent as she had said. If there was no connection between the two, then it was one of the strangest coincidences Blake had ever encountered. But if it had not been sheer coincidence —if the danger into which he had walked, or, rather, driven, had a connection with the visions he had seen in the crystal, then what did it mean?

It meant that the influence behind Thruster Joe might have been Dr. Huxton Rymer. And, remembering the past, Blake certainly had to admit that the manner of his shanghaiing undoubtedly was of the type of ruthless coup which Rymer would conceive.

If that connection were so, then what about the other?

Did it mean that Rymer had any connection with the shareholders' meeting of the Universal Machine Company? If he had, then was it not possible to go a step farther and seek for some association between Rymer and the absconding manager, Whidden Crane? At this time Blake knew nothing of the secret formula which had also been taken. But, even without that he knew that the enormous amount of loot which Crane had got away with, was quite sufficient to tempt Rymer.

It seemed too unreal, too fantastic to be submitted to the test of cold logic, but he had to admit that it was certainly a very strange coincidence—if that was all it was.

A different deck-hand attended Blake on the second day, and once again he tried to get the man to speak. His efforts were directed towards getting a message through to the captain; but as the man simply attended to his duties and refused to answer, Blake could not tell whether he was making any progress or not.

At night the same man appeared again, and this time Blake, who spoke modern Greek fluently, tried a different tack, playing on what he knew was the dominating trait of the Greek character.

That trait was the racial passion for money, for, probably, it would be almost impossible to find a race possessing more cupidity. When the man had completed his duties, he started for the ladder which led to the hatch, and Blake thought that once more his efforts had been fruitless. The deck-hand climbed the rungs until his head was above the hatch coaming, then, after a cautious look round, he descended again into the hold.

"What do you want?" he asked hurriedly.

"I want you to untie my hands or loosen the knots," answered Blake quickly. "I will pay you well for it."

Rarely did Blake have to confess himself beaten in this way, but on this occasion the ropes had been tied by sailors— experts at the game.

"How can you pay?" questioned the seaman. "You haven't any money. If you had, it has been taken away from you."

"Never mind. I will pay. I promise, you on the word of an Englishman. If you will do as I ask, I will give you fifty pounds."

"But how can you give it to me? If you try to escape, you will be killed."

"I will not be killed. And I will give it to you. I will send it to you, or leave it in London any place you say. I promise on my honour. "

"Wait," said the man with that he climbed back up the ladder, and Blake heard the hatch cover rattle into place.

Sexton Blake felt hands working at his bonds. Then the seaman's voice said : "Leave the money at the address in London if you get away. But no matter what happens, don't say I did it!" (*Chapter 8.*)

The Eighth Chapter.   When Greek Meets Coin —Rushing the Bridge —Blake Holds All the Cards —A Game of Bluff —Which Comes Off—Post Haste Back to Tinker.

WHAT time elapsed before Sexton Blake next heard a faint sound he did not know; but it seemed like hours. His ears were strained with long listening, and when at last he heard a faint scraping noise, he was doubtful whether it was a real sound or merely the product of his imagination.

At last it grew somewhat louder. This time he was sure. It was a sound that seemed to come from near at hand. It grew plainer and plainer until, suddenly, he realised that someone was creeping towards him over the boxes. A few minutes later he felt a touch on his arm. He turned over, and then fingers began to work at his bonds. Suddenly he felt them slip, and the next moment a piece of paper was thrust into his hand.

"Leave the money at that address in London if you get away. But no matter what happens, don't say I did it."

"I promise," whispered Blake, and lay quiet while the man crept away through the darkness.

When the sound no longer reached him, Blake sat up and chafed his cramped limbs. He untied the rope which bound his ankles, and ever so slowly stood upright, working his joints gingerly as he did so. For a good quarter of an hour he went through gentle exercise until his muscles had lost some of their ache.

Then he crept along over the boxes towards the iron ladder that led to the hatch. He climbed noiselessly until, by reaching up, he could touch the hatch cover. He pressed gently, and, to his satisfaction, found that the board yielded. Ever so gently he pushed until he was able to thrust it aside.

He screwed his head through and gazed about him.

It was night, with scarcely any sea running, and the dingy tramp was wallowing along at what Blake made to be about nine knots. Forward in the galley and in the passage leading to the fo'c's'le he could see lights.

From some place there, the sound of an accordion reached him. Looking up, he could see no sign of stars overhead. In what part of sea he was he had no idea, but he thought it highly probable that the tramp was crossing the Bay of Biscay. Up above him was the low bridge which was Blake's objective, but he could not make out any figures on it.

While he peered about him he was startled by the sudden clang of the bell. He counted four strokes, and put it down as ten o'clock. He wriggled through the opening, and slipped the cover back into place. Then he stole along the deck towards the ladder which led up to the bridge. Hand over hand he went up until his head was nearly level with the rail. He paused for a moment there, listening; then, with a sudden brisk decision, he went over the rail, landing with a thud not two yards from the man who was at the wheel.

Through the porthole of a small chart-room at the back Blake caught sight of a figure seated at a table. He recognised it as that of the dirty skipper who had accompanied Thruster Joe. On the table was a bottle and glass, and it was plain that the man was indulging in his favourite form of indoor amusement.

Before the startled man at the wheel could do anything, Blake was across the bridge and through the door into the chart-room. Without the slightest warning he hurled himself upon the seated figure at the table, and with a cry of amazed fear the captain came to his feet with one of his arms jammed up hard between his shoulder blades.

Blake dragged him away from the table and with his free hand felt the others pockets.

As he had hoped, he found what he wanted —a heavy revolver. With this in his hand he hurled the Greek clear, and when that astounded individual recovered himself he found himself looking into the barrel of his own weapon.

"Now, you crooked dog, one word out of you and I'll drill you clean!" snapped Blake. As he spoke he slammed the door of the chart-room and moved across to where he could command the bridge should anyone try to enter from there. "Sit down!" he snarled.

The Greek obeyed.

"Now you will answer my questions, and answer them without any cursed lies," went on Blake. "Let me warn you, you Levantine scum, that you have never been nearer death in your life than at this moment. Now then, what is the name of this ship?"

"The Corthos," answered the Greek sullenly.

"Bound for where?"

"Jaffa."

"What is her present position?"

"Off Finisterre."

"How much were you paid to shanghai me?"

For a moment the Greek hesitated, but Blake cocked the pistol in a significant way that caused the other to blurt out:

"Five hundred pounds."

"Who hired you to do the job?"

"I don't know. I was paid the money and no questions were to be asked."

"A pretty crook you are! What was to be my ultimate fate?"

"I was to turn you loose some place in the East."

"Are you equipped with wireless?"

"No."

"Call out to the man at the wheel and tell him to send word for your mate to come here —if you have one."

The Greek captain, now thoroughly under Blake's domination, obeyed. They sat thus for some minutes until there came a rap at the door and a swarthy man entered. He started back as he saw Blake standing over the captain with the revolver, but, at a gesture from Blake, he came inside.

"Are you the mate of this ship?" asked Blake curtly in the man's own language.

"Yes."

"You knew that I was a prisoner in the forward hold?"

"Yes."

"And how much did you get for your share in this?"

"I don't know what you mean. You are an enemy of my country, and we were taking you back to stand your trial."

"Is that what the captain told you?"

"Yes. It is true!"

"It is a lie. If you are telling the truth, then your captain has lied to you. Do you know that I am a British subject with a considerable amount of influence?"

The mate looked uneasy.

Blake turned to the captain. "Is he telling the truth?" he asked.

The Greek nodded.

"Then tell him the real facts!" snapped Blake. "And hurry up."

Haltingly the Greek revealed the truth. When he had finished Blake turned back to the mate.

"You know enough of International law to know just what sort of a noose you are running your neck in. If anything had happened to me my agents in London would have published their inquiries in every country in the world. They would also have offered a very heavy reward for information, and you can be sure that someone of your crew would have suspected the truth and told it.

"Now I propose to dictate certain terms. You can choose whether you accept them or not. If you do not, I can promise you that before you get past Gibraltar you will be overhauled by a British cruiser.

"You have heard the truth from this scum, who is unfit to command anything except a slave galley. You have heard the truth regarding the outrage that has been perpetrated on a British subject. You know what that means. If you obey my instructions you will escape the penalty. If not, you go before a British court to answer for your share in the affair."

The mate was thoroughly frightened, for now that he realised how the captain had hoodwinked him, and grasped that instead of having as a prisoner a renegade without a country, as the captain had said, they had outraged an influential British subject, he would sooner have handled live coals than take any further part in the affair.

"I will do whata you say," he stuttered.

"Then first, you will have this man" —and Blake pointed to the captain— "put in irons. Afterwards you will lay your course for Lisbon, which is the nearest port. Do you understand?"

"Yes."

"Then get busy!"

And, despite the curses and protests of the Greek captain, Blake's instructions were carried out. He forced the mate to explain the truth to the crew, and clinched that part of it by informing them how much the captain had received for his share. Next, Blake had the Greek thrust down into the hold from which he himself had escaped, and after that ordered the mate to issue instructions for a meal to be served in the cabin.

The latter, who was filled with a wholesome fear, obeyed, and after a personal investigation of the course they were making, and a comparison with the position as at midday that day, Blake retired to the chart-room and lighted a cigar.

Thus it was that, single-handed, he had captured the Greek tramp, and thirty hours later he had the satisfaction of seeing the tramp nose her way in towards the coast just above Lisbon. Blake remained on the tramp until an urgent message had brought the British vice-consul hastening to meet him. Half an hour later the Greek captain was taken off under arrest, and after rewarding the deck-hand who had released him, Blake followed with the vice-consul.

At that hospitable gentleman's house he was fitted with a complete change, and then, after securing funds, caught the express for Madrid. From Madrid he travelled by the Madrid-Paris express, reaching the French capital in exactly thirty-six hours. From Paris he motored to Le Bourget, where he caught an early morning plane for Croydon.

And that was how, a few minutes after ten o'clock he startled Tinker by entering the consulting-room at Baker Street so soon after the lad had read the cable from Bryant Kennedy in America.

NOT allowing Tinker much time to indulge in the amazement he felt on his dramatic re-appearance. Blake bundled him out of his seat, and dropping into his chair, said curtly:

"Now, then, Tinker, give me as quickly and as briefly as possible a complete resume of what has occurred here since my departure."

Blake's worn and haggard appearance told the lad plainly that his master had been through a pretty strenuous time, wherever he had spent his days since his mysterious disappearance from Baker Street, and he would have liked, more than anything, to allay the anxiety Blake's condition caused him.

But the latter's tone told him he would be wise to stick to the commands he had received, so pulling up a chair, he drew towards him the big pile of papers which had accumulated, and, in an emotionless tone, began his recital.

He dealt, firstly, with routine matters, adding a remark each time as to how he had dealt with it. Then he touched on the visit he had received from Sir Frederick Cameron, and explained how perturbed the latter had been at Blake's continued absence.

From that, the lad went on to explain how he had gone round to discuss things with Yvonne, and how, through a chance remark of Graves, he had found that Blake had apparently sailed from Havre for New York on the Orleans.

Following that, he detailed his further movements up to the time when he had cabled to Bryant Kennedy, and wound up his statement by handing Blake the cable he had received a few minutes before from Kennedy.

As Blake laid it down, Tinker added:

"When I saw in the list of passengers that Rymer, under the name of Professor Butterfield, was also on the Orleans, I thought that something had suddenly come up that had caused you to go off after him. But then, when I sent you a wireless and got the reply, of which I have already told you, I was all at sea. Mademoiselle Yvonne said she did not think the person on the Orleans could be you, and now I know, she was right."

"So Yvonne said that, did she?" cut in Blake, speaking for the first time since the lad had begun his recital. "What made her guess that?"

"She said it was just instinct, guv'nor. She —she has been very worried about you, guv'nor."

Blake made no reply, but motioned for Tinker to proceed.

"There isn't much more to tell," he went on. "We were marking time waiting to hear from Kennedy, and when I received this cable this morning, I didn't know what to do. I was just on the point of ringing up Mademoiselle Yvonne when you walked in. Where have you been, guv'nor?"

"I'll tell you later, my lad," said Blake, in softer tones. He realised now the deep anxiety Tinker must have been experiencing. "You may take it that I have been where it was impossible to communicate with Baker Street —at least, it was impossible until three days ago, and I had my reasons for lying low. Now I am going to do some telephoning. I want you to look up the sailings for New York. Find out how soon a steamer is going —it doesn't matter what line so long as it is a fast boat."

Wonderingly, Tinker jumped up to obey, while Blake took down the receiver. Tinker heard him call what he knew was Scotland Yard, and then, while he studied the sailing-lists in the morning paper, he heard Blake speaking to Inspector Thomas.

"There is an old acquaintance of yours, inspector, that I should be obliged if you will gather in. I, personally, will make the necessary charges against him. Yes —yes. Thruster Joe. Yes. You will find him in Poplar —or, at least, he was there about a week ago. He has been hanging out at the tenements over the inn. You know the place? I think he is good for a five or seven years this time, inspector.

"Thanks—if you will put one of your men on the job. And, inspector, with reference to the disappearance of one Whidden Crane. I believe you have that matter in hand. You have found no traces of him yet? Well, neither have I, but I am going after him, and I want a warrant to use, if necessary.

"Will you give me the necessary authority, in case I need it? For private reasons I am giving this precedence over all other matters. I am receiving no retaining fee other than actual expenses; but I have no doubt the company in question will pay a reward for the apprehension of Crane, and I promise you that the first hint of his whereabouts will go to you. And that means the reward.

"And now another favour, inspector. I want another warrant, in case I need it. The name —it is one that you will recall with little difficulty —Dr. Huxton Rymer. No —nothing that I can tell you now —a private case. Can I have them to-night? You will bring them on. Thank you!"

With that, Blake turned to find Tinker standing at his elbow.

"The Bretonic sails from Liverpool to-morrow at midday, guv'nor. There is a boat express from Euston at five o'clock in the morning."

"That will do us," said Blake. "'Get busy, my lad, and book a couple of berths. Pack some luggage this afternoon, and get everything ready. I am going to lie down now. I haven't had any sleep for days. You might also get through to Sir Frederick Cameron and ask him if I can see him this afternoon. As soon as you return from the shipping office wake me. I want to get an urgent cable away to Bryant Kennedy."

"But what about Mademoiselle Yvonne, guv'nor? Aren't you going to let her know that you have returned? She has been working with me, and she has been awfully worried."

Blake hesitated, then flushed slowly.

"I will attend to that, Tinker," he said.

And with that the lad had to be content. As soon as he had gone Blake sat down once more at the desk and gave the number of Yvonne's offices in Oxford Street. Miss Bryan, Yvonne's secretary answered, and, on Blake's inquiry, told him that Yvonne was in. A moment later Blake heard Yvonne's voice, trembling a little.

"You —you have returned," she said stammeringly.

"Yes, and I am leaving in the morning by the Bretonic for New York. But before I leave, I want to tell you, Yvonne, that I greatly appreciate what you did to assist Tinker. Also, I want to say that I am sorry for an incident that occurred the day I left."

"Please don't mention that again. I —I want to forget it. I am glad you are back safely."

Yvonne barely whispered the last words before she hung up, and for a full minute Blake sat staring thoughtfully at nothing particular. Then he rose and stumbled along to his dressing-room, where he threw off his clothes and lurched through to his bed-room utterly dead beat.

He was asleep almost before his head touched the pillow, and thus it was that Tinker found him two hours later.

Nor did Blake know that, shortly after he had called up Yvonne, Tinker had arrived at the offices in Oxford Street, where he told Yvonne of Blake's appearance, and as much as he himself knew of his master's absence.

Despite his fatigue, Blake came up sitting as soon as Tinker touched his shoulder. After a cold plunge, he slipped into a loose flannel suit and made his way to the consulting-room, where a tremendous amount of work had to be disposed of before they left London.

Blake nodded when Tinker informed him that he had managed to secure a good cabin on the Bretonic, and that Sir Frederick Cameron would call at Baker Street about half-past five that evening. Then they settled down to make out a long code cable to Bryant Kennedy, which Tinker took out to send off. From that on, Blake worked at high pressure until Sir Frederick Cameron made his appearance.

To the baronet Blake did not reveal the reasons for his absence from London, but roused some hope in the other's mind when he informed him that he was off for New York in the morning, and thought he was on the track of the absconding manager.

Then they discussed, in some detail, the additional discovery of the missing formula, and Blake agreed with the chairman that it was highly probable that this had also been taken by Crane. Ever since Tinker had told him about this, Blake's mind had been subconsciously dwelling on the circumstance, and one conclusion he had come to— whether there was any connection between Rymer and Crane, or not, the existence of such a secret formula would be of intense interest to Rymer, who as a scientist, would appreciate to the full its value in the steel industry of any country.

They dined quietly at Baker Street, and afterwards returned to the consulting-room to work. They were so engaged when Inspector Thomas arrived.

"You are not looking very fit, Blake," he remarked, as he seated himself and took one of Blake's cigars. "Been overdoing things a bit lately?"

"A little, inspector," replied Blake carelessly. "Have you heard anything from the man you sent out after Thruster Joe?"

"I have. He found him just where you said he would be found. He must have been up to something pretty profitable lately. He had over seventy pounds on him when we searched him. What is the charge?"

"Criminal assault and abduction," answered Blake grimly.

"That will fix him for a term all right, if you can prove it. Who did he assault?"

Blake puffed in silence at his cigar. It was not easy for him to answer that question, for it was decidedly difficult for him to confess that he had walked into a trap, the type of which he looked upon as distinctly crude.

He had confessed to himself that it was due to a blunder on his part, but it was not easy to tell that to Inspector Thomas.

At the same time, Blake was out for a cold vengeance on those who had been the means of shipping him out of the country like a shanghaied Chink, and he knew he must take the fence of acknowledging that an unintelligent brute like Thruster Joe had gained an advantage over him.

He smiled.

"The person whom Thruster Joe assaulted and abducted was myself."

"You! You are joking!" exclaimed the inspector, while Tinker's eyes nearly popped out of his head.

"I am not joking. I am perfectly serious. I walked into a trap that was so wide open, I ought to have sensed it easily. But the fact remains that I did."

Inspector Thomas put his head back and laughed in deep enjoyment.

"My —my —my!" he chuckled. "That is the best thing I have heard for years! You taken in by Thruster Joe! Oh, won't they laugh at the Yard when I tell them that!"

"They might," admitted Blake, also smiling. "But I think they will regard the affair in a different light before I have finished with Thruster Joe and those who employed him."

The inspector grew serious.

"Exactly what is it, Blake?" he asked.

"Wait until you get over your enjoyment of the joke, inspector, then perhaps —perhaps I will tell you. Have you brought those warrants and authority for me to act?"

"Yes. I got them all fixed up."

As he spoke, the inspector took out a long blue envelope which he handed to Blake.

"Has this anything to do with the other affair?" he asked.

Blake laid the envelope on the desk.

"As I told you, inspector, I may perhaps tell you later on."

And then the inspector was sorry that he hadn't restrained his mirth until he had heard all Blake had to say. But as it was the first time for years that he had known of Blake being caught napping, he could not resist exhibiting his appreciation of the joke.

He little knew the events which had led up to Blake's being in such a state of mental concentration that it would have been strange, indeed, if he had not walked into the trap which had been so cunningly laid for him, and the very strength of which was its simplicity.

Blake got rid of the inspector as soon as he decently could; then he and Tinker settled down once more to work. It was well past midnight before Blake pushed the papers away from him and leant back.

"That will do for to-night, my lad," he said wearily. "I think we have brought things up to date as far as possible. Have you packed our luggage?"

"Yes, guv'nor, and I told Mrs. Bardell to serve tea at a quarter past four."

"All right, my lad. Now you had better cut along to bed. As it is, we shall only get about three hours' sleep."

"I will go at once, guv'nor. But, I say, won't you please tell me before I go where you have been and what happened to you?"

Blake lighted a cigarette, and, getting up, walked across to one of the deep saddlebag chairs.

"I will tell you, Tinker," he said in tired tones, "but you will not find it of much interest. I was quite honest with Inspector Thomas. I did blunder —badly. At what point do you wish me to begin?"

"Just where Mademoiselle Yvonne and I saw you leave the bazaar that afternoon, guv'nor. I haven't told you, but we drove through here after, and just as we turned into Baker Street we saw you —or, at least, then we thought it was you —drive away in the Grey Panther. From the investigations I made here some days later, I knew it couldn't have been you. But what happened, guv'nor?"

So Blake began, and as far as he could told Tinker just what had occurred from the time he left the bazaar until the moment when he had arrived back at Baker Street. As he related how for some days he had lain bound on the hard wooden cases which formed the cargo of the Greek tramp, the lad's eyes flashed with anger, and when he had finished, Tinker muttered:

"If we had only known that, guv'nor. There were you, going through a time like that, and we didn't know!"

Blake laughed softly as he tossed away the end of his cigarette and rose. He walked across, and laid his hand on Tinker's shoulder.

"You are a good lad, Tinker. Sometimes, when I am irritable or worried, I may speak abruptly. But, believe me, my lad, I should have been much more easy in my mind if it had been possible to have your loyal co-operation when I was tied up on board the Greek tramp.

"But this particular case must be fought out on its merits. I blame myself more than a little for walking into such a simple trap, but, at the same time, it has served to give me a lead —a lead that I shall follow, my lad, until someone goes to ground. Now let us go to bed!"

It was just a few minutes after half-past four the next morning when Blake and Tinker entered a taxi at Baker Street and drove through to Euston. They were travelling light —a couple of small cabin trunks, and two good-sized suitcases was all the luggage they had.

It was evident that the Bretonic was to receive a large contingent of passengers by the early morning boat-train, for the platform was crowded when they arrived.

When their luggage had been put in the van, Blake, who was trying to read an early morning edition, followed Tinker along to where the lad said he had secured a carriage. He stood aside for Blake to climb in. Blake noticed casually that the carriage was already occupied by two ladies, but with a formal lifting of his hat he paid them no further attention. He became once more engrossed in his paper; but if he had happened to glance at Tinker, he would have wondered what could be amusing the lad so. It was not until the train was pulling out that Blake heard a very sweet and familiar voice say:

"Is he always as cross as this in the mornings, Tinker?"

Blake dropped the paper to his knees, and turned in amazement. He saw a pair of laughing eyes gazing roguishly at him over a black fur against which a big bunch of parma violets nestled.

"Yvonne! Why—why —What on earth are you doing here?" he stammered.

Yvonne laughed again.

"I?" she said. "Why, I am going to New York by the Bretonic."

Blake glanced at her companion, and saw that it was Anna, Yvonne's maid. Next his eyes took in her dressing-case and rugs, and he knew that she was not joking. Then he shot a shrewd glance at the grinning Tinker.

"Er —from the guilty look in Tinker's eye, I should say that he was already aware of that fact," he said, with a smile.

"Yes. We thought you really needed looking after."

And even Blake read the look of deep concern in Yvonne's eyes as she studied his careworn countenance.

Needless to say, it became a very jolly party from that on, and if Yvonne had any doubts about the wisdom of her decision to cross to New York by the Bretonic, she would have found a very satisfactory answer had she been able to hear the song that was singing in Blake's heart.

Never, probably, had he felt more deeply appreciative of those who meant so much in his life than at that moment.

The Tenth Chapter.   On the Bretonic —Kennedy Gets Some Facts —A Trans-Continental Chase —A Race Against Time —At San Francisco —A Vital Ten Minutes —Too Late.

BRETONIC slipped down the Mersey sharp on the hour. When the tiny tugs had finished puffing importantly about her, and the wide mouth of the river opened up, she got under full way, and by the time lunch in the big restaurant was over, the great liner was already ploughing through the Irish sea.

Her last voyage had been an Atlantic record, the time being just a trifle under five days between New York and Liverpool. It was rumoured aboard that the captain was out to smash his own record, and this suited Blake's plans perfectly, for with him time was a very essential factor.

All he knew for certain was that someone, calling himself Sexton Blake, had sailed for New York by the Orleans. He knew, further, that on the same boat had been Dr. Huxton Rymer. Beyond that he had only the tentative hypothesis he had formed while lying bound in the dark hold of the Greek tramp.

That hypothesis had been built on nothing stronger than the foundation Blake had been able to hammer out with his own common-sense and logical mind from what might seem a mad suggestion —the hazy visions he had seen in the crystal of the psychic. And yet, since his return to London, he had been able to pick up more than one loose thread; and, while he did not confide fully in either Yvonne or Tinker, he was determined to run to earth the two men who had travelled by the Orleans.

He knew that one was Rymer; he thought the other might be Whidden Crane. But what connection there was between the two, if any, he didn't even attempt to guess.

Owing to heavy seas and strong head winds, the Bretonic did not succeed in smashing her own record, but even at that she arrived in New York just a little over five days from the time she had dropped down the Mersey.

Two days out of New York, Blake had received a long code wireless from Bryant Kennedy, which had told him that Kennedy had sent out word broadcast to carry out the instructions Blake had cabled from London. They had scarcely docked before Kennedy himself came up the gangway and sought Blake. He had, of course, met both Yvonne and Tinker before, and after greeting them, drew Blake aside.

"I am afraid I haven't been able to find out as much as you would have wished, Blake, but I have some news for you."

"What is it, Kennedy?" asked Blake quickly.

"This. I have been able to trace your man, Professor Butterfield. At least, I have traced him as far as Chicago. My men there are on his heels, and I expect word any minute as to his movements. He certainly has a companion travelling with him, but not under your name. That is where I am a little at sea."

"That is more than I had hoped for, Kennedy. Have you been able to get any trace of the man who travelled on my name and passport?"

"Absolutely nothing. In my opinion, Blake, he dropped it as soon as he landed here."

Blake nodded.

"How about a new passport?"

"Easy enough. There are half a dozen men here in New York who can copy any passport and vise that was ever written."

"Then what about the companion who is travelling with Professor Butterfield? Mightn't it be the same man?"

"In my opinion, it must be. But I wanted to hear what you thought before suggesting that."

"If they are only in Chicago now, then they could have spent several days here in New York. We might get a little light on that when you hear further from your men in Chicago. At any rate, we can't do anything for the moment. Will you come along and dine with us? I suppose you got rooms for us at the Belmont?"

"Yes —and I have a car waiting for you. I shall be glad to dine, but I must go along to the office first."

They rejoined Yvonne and Tinker then, and, thanks to Kennedy, were passed through the Customs with the barest formalities. Kennedy had a big twelve cylinder Packard waiting for them, and, after seeing their luggage into a taxi, they entered the car. It was just after five when they pulled out of the dock into Tenth Avenue, and, on reaching the Belmont, Yvonne went up at once to her rooms with Anna trailing behind with numerous small bags and cases.

They did not meet again until after seven in the lounge, and when Yvonne came down, looking like a lovely flower in her soft dinner-frock of some filmy emerald green material, she found Blake,

Kennedy and Tinker standing together, talking earnestly.

She asked no questions, but when Blake had ordered dinner, he leant across to Yvonne and whispered:

"Kennedy has heard from his Chicago agents. Our men left to-day for San Francisco."

"And what will you do now?" murmured Yvonne.

"Tinker and I leave for San Francisco to-morrow. Kennedy's agents will keep us posted on the way."

Suddenly Blake reached out and took from between Yvonne's fingers a tiny cinnamon rose, which she had been idly twisting about.

"And you, Yvonne," he said, in a low tone. "What will you do?"

Yvonne lifted her long lashes and gazed at Blake for one brief moment, then the deep violet of her eyes was suddenly veiled.

"I —oh, I suppose I shall stay for a few days in New York, and then return to England."

"Have you any important engagements there?"

"N-no."

"You seem to hesitate. Is Paul Brabazon still in London?"

"I believe so."

"I understand, then."

"Man of wondrous penetration," murmured Yvonne. "What is it you understand?"

Blake crushed the harmless little rose.

"Why. I understand—" he began, when just then Tinker's voice interrupted him.

"I say. Mademoiselle Yvonne," said Tinker, "you are coming through to 'Frisco with us. aren't you? It would be awfully jolly if you could manage it."

Yvonne smiled into Tinker's eyes. "Why, thank you, Tinker, I should love to come,"

And Sexton Blake, with a vague feeling that he was out of his depth, lifted his cocktail and drained it at a single gulp.

They left for Chicago the next day, and on their arrival there Blake received confirmation from Kennedy's Chicago agent that he was on the right trail. Professor Butterfield had been traced to the St. Charles' Hotel, in 'Frisco, and had booked his passage by the Venezuela, which was to sail for the East in five days' time. With him, still, was a companion, whose name Kennedy's sleuths had given as Gilbert Crawford, although no description was as yet available.

This, however, was something to go on, and that same night Blake, Tinker, and Yvonne, with Anna in tow, boarded the North-Western train on a race against time, for, according to the schedule of running, they should arrive in 'Frisco just two hours before the Venezuela was due to sail.

It was a pleasant enough journey through the Corn Belt country, but it began to get monotonous and tiring when they hit the sage bush plains of the Far West; and, when, in the heavy summer heat, they crossed the Great Salt Lake of Utah, they were looking forward eagerly to the foothills of the Rockies, which they would reach in Nevada.

From there on, it was a journey of wondrous beauty — the long climb through the heavy timber and mighty gorges of the Rockies, the fleeting glimpses of beautiful lakes, set like jewels in the lap of the mighty peaks, the long, dingy line of snow sheds, with their gloom and broken flashes of light, then the passing of the summit at more than eight thousand feet, and, after that, the swift descent to Sacramento, and the palms.

From Sacramento, on down through the Santa Barbara valley, Blake was continually consulting his watch. At Sacramento they had been running an hour and a half behind time, due to engine trouble at Truekee on the summit. But the conductor had assured Blake that they would make this up before they got to Berkeley.

At Berkeley, however, they had only cut it down a bare twelve minutes, and, when Blake thought of the slow ferry journey across to 'Frisco from Oakland, his brows drew down. At Oakland they had lost the twelve minutes and another seven as well.

There the train was split up into sections, and run on to the train ferry which would take them across to 'Frisco.

Blake paced up and down impatiently, until, after what seemed an eternity, they finally cast off. As they drew out into San Francisco Bay, his eyes swept across the grey waters past the two islands, and on towards the bend which led to the Golden Gate.

Mighty Tamalpais had no attractions for him then, nor did the misty blue of the distant ranges hold his gaze. His whole mind was concentrated on just one thing—to reach the Venezuela before she sailed.

When the train ferry had pulled into the wharf at the foot of

Market Street, Blake pushed a way through the crowd, and guided his party along to where the public automobiles were parked. Into one he packed Anna with the luggage, giving the driver instructions to go to the Fairmont Hotel and wait his arrival. Into another, he, Yvonne, and Tinker climbed, and, at Blake's urging, the machine tore along Market Street towards the Pacific Mail pier. Arriving there, it took Blake just one minute to discover that the Venezuela had sailed less than ten minutes before. As he climbed back into the car, he said to the driver:

"Make it through Golden Gate Park as quickly as you can. Pull up at point near the Seal Rocks."

Yvonne and Tinker knew without being told what had happened, but neither of them spoke to Blake just then. Each knew, from an entirely different phase of understanding, just what Blake was feeling.

They sat without speaking while the driver broke all traffic laws by tearing through the city to the park. There he drove at a terrific pace, until suddenly the thick firs thinned out, and just ahead of them lay the bay. To the left was the Golden Gate with, in the middle distance, the famous Seal Rocks.

Through the Golden Gate, from far across the mighty Pacific, came a wide golden lane, thrown out in gentle caress by the dying sun. And then, suddenly, across the path of gold swept a mighty shape.

Blake watched it broodingly as it surged along that lane of gold, tossing aside the glistening nuggets with prodigal indifference. Straight towards the Golden Gate it ploughed its way, growing smaller and smaller, each moment until it became dwarfed by the mighty sentinels which guard the entrance to the bay. Then, even as the sun dipped slowly into the distant horizon, it met the heave of the outer ocean and was gone.

Blake turned away, and drew out his cigarette-case.

"Too late," he said quietly. "Our friends have gone into the West with the whole Pacific before them."

"What will you do?" asked Yvonne gently.

Blake gazed once more through the Golden Gate.

"What will I do?" he repeated more to himself than in answer to Yvonne. His jaw set like steel "What will I do?" he said once more; "I will follow them, and rake the whole Pacific from the Aleuts to

Easter Island, and from America to the Moluccas, if necessary, for here I vow that I shall not return to London until I have laid that pair by the heels."

And watching his eyes, now hard as steel points, both Yvonne and Tinker knew that Blake would keep his word.

THE END.
[22400 WORDS]

U.J.—No. 981.